Wings of Olympus

of

THE COLT OF THE CLOUDS

Wings of Olympus

of

THE COLT OF THE CLOUDS

BY

KALLIE GEORGE

HARPER

An Imprint of HarperCollinsPublishers

Author's Note

Throughout this book, in most names, "k" is used
instead of a "c," as that is the Greek form of spelling,
whereas a "c" would be Roman. However, Hercules
we have here spelled with a "c" because it is the most
commonly used version of the hero's name.

Wings of Olympus: The Colt of the Clouds
Text copyright © 2020 by Kallie George
HarperCollins Children's Books, a division of HarperCollins Publishers, 195 Broadway,
New York, NY 10007.
www.harpercollinschildrens.com
ISBN 978-0-06-274154-7
Typography by Joe Merkel
20 21 22 23 24   PC/LSCH   10 9 8 7 6 5 4 3 2 1
❖
First Edition

To Orion, named after the stars—K. G.

*I*n a cave thick with shadows, in the deepest depths of Mount Olympus, she sat restlessly on her throne, her wings wrapped around her. It was not yet night, and for her this meant a chance to sleep. But she couldn't. Something was bothering her.

Someone was bothering her.

He stood before her and bowed, humbly. They were all humble before her—all the other gods and goddesses—for she had been there long before they were even born. Why, she had birthed the gods—at least, a good many of them.

"Help me," he pleaded.

"Why should I help you?" she replied.

"Because . . ." He reached into his chiton, shimmering like an abalone shell, and pulled out a feather, presenting it to her. It was long and silver and bright as a star. A feather from Pegasus, the first winged horse, who had long since retired to the night sky as one of her constellations. "Because of this."

She took the feather thoughtfully. She imagined them all, how dazzling her cloak would be, far brighter than her daughter's. And though she had vowed never to work for anyone but herself, she surprised herself with her answer.

"So be it," she said.

One

Above the rolling fields of Thessaly, clouds wisped across the sky like horses' tails. In the distance, toward Mount Olympus, Pippa could see darker, thicker ones gathering, but she didn't pay them any attention, too focused on the task at hand.

She hoisted another rock to fill in the hole in the pasture wall, wiping her hands on her *chiton*. She knew she shouldn't dirty it, but sometimes she forgot. It's why she preferred a short tunic rather than this chiton or the fancy embroidered *peplos* that Helena liked her to wear.

"You don't have to help me with this," said Bas, wiping sweat from his brow. The sun was still shining, despite the hint of a coming storm.

"I want to," Pippa said. It was this or lessons. Helena, Bas's mother, was waiting for her to continue with their weaving before she had to oversee supper preparations. Pippa would rather lift a thousand rocks than twist and tangle her fingers in yarn. She wished she were better at it like Bas's sisters, or at least liked it better. But she didn't. And that made things worse.

"Well, we're almost done anyway," said Bas, then added ruefully, "until the next time."

The wild horses had broken the fence more than once now to get to the old stables, unused except for storing surplus hay. Pippa didn't really mind. She liked the wild horses that streaked free across the sun-washed hills of Thessaly, their bodies small and sturdy, their manes and tails tangled with twigs and leaves.

She had seen them only a handful of times when she was out riding with her horse, Zephyr, but was pleased whenever she did. They didn't have wings like Zeph once had, yet they were special too, and carried themselves with the same pride.

"*Feral* horses, not wild," Bas's father liked to correct. "They ran away from a farm like mine, years and years ago."

But to Pippa, they were wild—wild and free.

"Done," declared Bas, putting the last piece of rubble in place.

The fence looked taller than before, stretching seemingly without end along the rolling pasture. In the distance, Pippa could see Zeph grazing, his silvery-white tail swishing rhythmically. Farther away were the other horses. They liked to keep their distance from Zeph, although so far he had caused no problems, not even with the mares. Beyond the horses was the *oikos*, the house, its sunbaked brick glowing golden in the afternoon light.

Pippa glanced at Bas and understood his proud smile.

After she had returned with him from the race on Mount Olympus and had seen it all for the first time—the pastures, the stables, the grand house with its courtyard big enough to enclose an olive tree—she knew at once how wealthy Bas's family must be. Only the wealthy, the *hoi aristoi*, could afford horses. Suddenly, she had been afraid to meet his family. Would they really want to take in a foundling like her, especially one with a horse to feed as well?

"I have plenty of sisters. What's one more?" Bas had said reassuringly. "My family will love you. You have a way with horses."

She *did* have a way with horses. But people were more of a puzzle. Bas was one of her two true friends, along with Sophia, who had won the Winged Horse Race and now lived on Mount Olympus with the gods.

Still, Pippa needn't have worried. Bas had been right; his family had welcomed her with open arms. To them, she wasn't a foundling, she was a rider, chosen by Aphrodite, the goddess of love. And Zeph—he was a winged horse. Even without his wings, he was instantly a legend. So everything was fine. At least, at first. . . .

Bas ran his hand through his dark hair. "I should find my father and tell him we're done." He paused. "Are you coming?"

"In a bit," said Pippa, gazing fondly back at Zeph.

Bas gave her a reproachful look. "You're thinking of riding, aren't you?"

Pippa shook her head.

But, of course, that's exactly what she was thinking.

* * *

The moment Bas was out of sight, Pippa hurried to the stables to pocket some figs. They were Zeph's favorite. If she was quick, she and Zeph could be back before the storm. Helena wouldn't have time to notice that Pippa was gone.

When she reached Zeph out in the pasture, he was as eager as she. His silver tail was lifted high and seemed to float in the wind. His forelock stuck up too, like a tiny horn, and she smoothed it down. She hadn't brought a saddlecloth or reins. With Zeph, she didn't need any.

Quickly, she vaulted onto his back, a move that took strength but had become second nature for Pippa. Then they were off.

They rode past the fields of olive trees and barley that grew green and gold beside the river. Past the vineyards, where the grapevines were just beginning to bud. Past the other farmhouses that glowed with the last slips of sun. Soon they entered the small town and the *agora*, the marketplace, where lyre music filled the air and servants and slaves haggled with traders and stallholders over the price of cheese and olives, eggs and bread. Children scurried by—laughing, rolling hoops

with sticks, and pulling each other in toy chariots—
but when they saw Pippa and Zeph, they stopped to
stare and whisper. Everyone in town knew about her
and Zephyr, the winged horse without wings.

In the center of town, on a rise, Pippa could see the
temple built to honor Zeus, king of the gods, although
none but the oracles and priests could go there. Soon,
she'd passed through the town and was back into the
countryside, the cobblestone road turning to dirt.

The sun warmed her cheeks, and she breathed in
the sweet, fresh smell of river and earth, horse and hay.
Nearby, the water lapped at the river's banks. The gentle *clip-clop* of Zeph's hooves and lullaby swish of his
tail made Pippa beam with pleasure. There was nothing she wouldn't do for him.

She pressed her legs into his sides, coaxing him to
gallop quickly by the hut of the old crone Leda, who
watched everything with the acuity of Argus, the
many-eyed giant. If Leda saw Pippa pass, she would
no doubt report to Helena as soon as she could. There
were lots of old women in the village, but none as
grouchy as Leda. No one knew much about her, except
to stay away. Although she loved to poke into other
people's business, she kept her own past as hidden as

her hair beneath her *himation*, the woolen cloak that she never left the house without.

Before long they came to a fork in the path. One way led to the next town, the other toward the hills.

"To the hills," Pippa decided aloud. She had spent many an hour exploring the forests in this area, and the way to the hills was prettiest.

She knew she should head back, but the sooner she returned, the sooner the lessons began. Missing a lesson meant more weaving and spinning the next day. There was no avoiding it.

She tightened her grip on Zeph's mane. He snorted, and his shoulders shuddered in a strange way that only his did. Often Pippa wondered if he was still trying to flex his wings. She had watched him carefully those first few weeks after he had lost them to see how much he missed flying. But even now he seemed, two years later, to be happy.

But was she?

Before she had a chance to think further on this, the ground shook and a loud crack filled the air. *Thunder.*

Pippa glanced at the sky. The thick, dark clouds were directly overhead now, so it almost felt like night but starless. Again thunder cracked, this time so loud it made Pippa jump. Zeph froze, his ears pricked.

When the thunder was this mighty, Zeus had to be near. Pippa searched the sky for a lightning bolt, for a flash of wing or hoof. But there was nothing. No sign of Zeus, or his winged steed, Ajax, the winner of the most recent Winged Horse Race.

Pippa sighed, as Zeph, his ears still on the alert, continued along the path to the meadows of blossoms and stones. She would love to see a winged horse again. All she had was a single feather she'd kept from Zeph's wings. She had gotten the idea from Zeus, who kept a feather from Pegasus, his first winged steed, pinned on his cloak.

It seemed so long ago now since the race. She wasn't sure if Zeph missed flying, but she did.

It was a secret she told no one, not even Bas. He wouldn't understand. He hadn't wanted to stay on Mount Olympus. He had missed his family too much. Besides, there was nothing she could do about how she felt. She and Bas had been banished from the mountain, from the winged horses. That was their punishment for having cheated, switching horses on the morning of the race.

And there was no hope of her being chosen for the

Winged Horse Race again, since not only was she banished but also the race occurred only once every hundred years. Maybe her daughter—no, granddaughter . . . But that meant Pippa would have to marry, and then she'd spend even more time weaving and cooking and washing, all the things that women were supposed to do. All the things she had never learned because she had no mother. She bit her lip. This was the reason for the lessons from Helena. Bas had lessons too, only his were with a tutor who taught him how to read and write.

Pippa could just imagine her friend Sophia being outraged at the difference. Sophia loved books and studying more than anything. Now that she was a demigoddess on Mount Olympus, she could take part in lessons with boys. She could *teach* boys, for that matter.

Sometimes Pippa wondered if all Bas's sisters really were as pleased with their places in life as they made out to be. If they weren't, they didn't share it with her. She certainly knew that Astrea, the youngest, loved horses almost as much as she did and was often found playing in the stables, much to Helena's dismay.

Pippa sighed and stuck her hand in the pocket of her peplos, touching her coin, the only thing she had left from her parents. They'd abandoned her when she was a baby. For a long time, Pippa had thought the coin—silver with a winged horse on it—was an *obolos*, a coin that was given to those left for dead, as fare for safe passage into the Underworld. But Aphrodite, who had been Pippa's patron during the race, had confirmed that it wasn't. It was a symbol of good luck; it meant she was loved. It was also a reminder that she was different. She should have insisted that Aphrodite find out more about her parents. Why had they abandoned her? But you couldn't insist upon anything when it came to the gods and goddesses. They did as they pleased.

Like now. What was Zeus up to?

The clouds roiled overhead, more turbulent than she'd ever seen. As the first few drops of rain fell, they tingled on her skin, making it prickle.

Strange, thought Pippa.

She stuck out her tongue to taste the droplets, only to snap it back in at once. This *wasn't* ordinary rain. It was salty!

Two

The rain poured down harder—great big drops—
pooling and puddling, soaking Pippa's hair and
dripping from Zeph's mane. Pippa tested it again,
licking the water from her hand, just to make sure.
Salty!

Storms didn't make salty rain. Something was
wrong. She shivered and looked up at the sky again,
trying to spot Zeus. But there was no sign of him, only
huge black clouds that looked like bruises in the sky.

"Come on, Zeph. Time to go home," Pippa said,
tugging on his mane.

But Zeph wouldn't move. His ears were pricked and his muscles taut.

"Come on," Pippa urged again. But instead of turning back toward the stables, he did the opposite, stepping forward, his ears swiveling this way and that, as though he could hear something she couldn't.

"No, Zeph," said Pippa, this time pressing her legs into his sides.

But her horse wouldn't listen. He took another step along the path.

Boom! The sound split the air and set the ground shaking with a force that felt more like an earthquake than thunder. Zeph reared, and Pippa tipped backward.

"Whoa!" she cried, pressing her body forward and frantically wrapping her arms around his neck.

When Zeph came down on all four feet, he took off, bolting along the path, his hooves churning the flooded earth to mud, and it took all Pippa's strength just to hang on. Her body slipped against his in the rain, and she could barely see as the salty drops drilled her eyes. He galloped so fast he seemed almost to hover, as though he had found his wings again.

The path twisted along the riverside, and soon the meadows turned to trees. Zeph sped between the pines and laurels, their branches trembling from the force of the deluge.

"Stop!" Pippa cried, but Zeph was like a different horse, a wild one who wouldn't listen to her, who didn't even know her.

Pippa knew he wasn't perfect. He was an easily distracted horse. That was why he was named after a zephyr, a breeze, because, as a winged horse, he had often darted and dallied like one. But he had never moved in such a determined, driven way, except perhaps during the race itself.

The branches flew by overhead, nearly knocking her off his back.

Enough was enough! She *had* to stop him.

She pulled back as hard as she could on his mane, but Zeph only shot forward faster, and this time Pippa couldn't keep her hold. She slid off, tumbling to the earth. She curled her body and landed on her side. *Thump!* Luckily, the muddy ground softened her fall.

Instantly, she sprang up. Zeph was already a silvery speck, streaking through the trees, blurred by the pouring rain.

"ZEPH!" she shouted. She ran after him, leaping over branches and roots of trees. The forest was dark and empty, as though the storm had frightened all the animals—the birds and boars and many others—into hiding.

Another boom of thunder shook the sky, and again the ground quaked. Pippa clutched a tree branch to keep her footing. A storm didn't cause earthquakes or salty rain. This was the gods expressing their anger. But at whom? She prayed to Aphrodite to keep her and Zeph safe.

Pippa was soaked now, her hair dripping into her eyes, her chiton sticking to her body. "Zeph! Zeph!" she cried. She listened but could hear only the pounding of the rain.

"ZEPH!" she cried again.

Was that a distant whinny?

She pressed on, through the trees, in the mud.

She heard the sound once more. It *was* a whinny. High-pitched and desperate.

Was he hurt?

"ZEPH!" she cried, her voice wobbling.

She ran even faster, slipping and falling and slipping again. Until, at last, the trees opened up and she emerged into a clearing.

Zeph!

Pippa let out a huge sigh of relief. She had found him! He wasn't hurt. There he circled, his coat slick with rain, in front of an old temple.

Pippa had heard of this old temple to Zeus, but she had never seen it, despite her many outings through the hills. The new one had been built long before she came to Thessaly.

Once, the temple might have been impressive and imposing, but now it looked anything but. Vines and moss grew between thickly between the columns. The roots of an oak tree had pushed up the stone steps, causing them to crumble. Gold and silver paint was peeling from the walls. And, worse, a column had collapsed inward on part of the roof, creating a mountain of white rubble. The damage looked recent, perhaps even caused by the storm.

Zeph paced and pawed, whinnying frantically.

All of a sudden, Pippa knew why.

From inside the temple, another horse whinnied back.

Three

Pippa's breath caught in her throat.

She stepped closer, until she was beside Zeph. She couldn't see the strange horse fully through the rubble and the relentless rain. Only a flash of silver mane and tail. A wild horse—it had to be! It must have been seeking shelter inside when the temple collapsed. Surely it could push its way through the vines on the other side. Unless it was trapped.

But then it gave another whinny—more like a shriek this time—and Pippa knew: it was panicked. A panicked horse was like a panicked person. Logic was forgotten.

Zeph turned to Pippa, snorting anxiously.

"How did you know?" Pippa asked. Zeph's starry eyes bore into hers, not answering, only pleading.

"Hush!" she cried to the horse, though she knew her words wouldn't help. She needed to *do* something.

She began to shift the rubble. The stones were hard to move, wet and slippery in the rain. Pippa managed to lift the first few, then roll some others out of the way. *Thud!* They fell, heavy, in the muck outside the temple. When a piece of stone was too big for Pippa to move on her own, Zeph helped, using his nose to push it aside.

Pippa talked to the horse as she worked, even though the roar of the rain drowned out her voice. "Shhh, shhh," she said, huffing. "It's okay."

At last, they'd cleared a hole just big enough for the horse to get out. She peered inside, but it was too dark and shadowy to see much.

"Here, come here," called Pippa as reassuringly as she could. "You're free now."

Zeph nickered as though repeating her words.

The horse snorted. Zeph did too. A small silver nose reached out to touch his.

Pippa let out a long, soft whistle and held out her

hand. The little horse took a step backward into the shadows. Pippa remembered the figs that she had pocketed for Zeph. She pulled one out and offered it.

Zeph snorted eagerly.

"Not for you," she chided.

She waited patiently, and at last the silver nose appeared again, followed by a face. Its nostrils flared out, wide and round as two *drachma* coins, and its ears flicked back and forth furiously. Its eyes were a deep, dreamy black, just like Zeph's but even blacker, if that was possible. It sniffed, and slowly . . . very slowly . . . it nosed her hand.

Its muzzle was soft, soft as clouds.

"Come on," she coaxed. As slow as sunbeams move across a meadow, the colt—for it *was* a colt—stepped out of the temple.

Buffeted by the rain and wind, the colt's whole body trembled, from his long legs and knobby knees to his . . .

Pippa gasped.

Wings. Two wings rose from his back, spindly and silver, with dustings of gold glittering like a starry sky. They were half folded, like delicate fans, but huge. Rain dripped from the long feathers, pooling at his hooves.

Winged horses weren't supposed to roam below Mount Olympus. It was a rule. That's why Zeph had lost his wings on the way down. Long ago, Bellerophon, on a quest to become a hero, had tamed Pegasus with a golden bridle, but when he had tried to ride the winged horse up to the palace of the gods, he'd nearly died. Bellerophon was now the immortal groom of Mount Olympus. But since then, no winged horses had touched mortal soil.

Until now.

Though the colt's wings were huge, the rest of him was small. He wasn't fully grown, although he wasn't as small as a foal either. A yearling, too old to need his mare but still too young to be by himself. He wasn't alone now. Zeph nosed the colt again, leaning his head down tenderly.

All at once, Pippa thought of the fence and the wild horses. So many times they had broken through. Maybe one of the mares had been breaking in for a reason—to see Zeph. It was the only explanation. And also explained why he was so eager to help. This was his *son*.

And his son was hurt.

Pippa's heart thrummed. She felt a surge of protective love.

She could see that the colt's left wing looked strange, held closer to his side than his right one. He was injured. Had a rock fallen on him?

"It's okay, little one," she said. She couldn't let him stay here; she had to bring him back. He needed a good meal—barley mash with beans—and someone to look after his injured wing. The rain still pummeled the earth.

She didn't have a lead rope, but she did have her belt, a long, thin piece of cloth that held her chiton in place. She took it off and tied a simple loop.

The colt retreated slightly, so she stuck her hand into the pocket of her chiton to get another fig.

She dropped it on the soggy ground. The colt sniffed and took a step forward. Quickly, he munched it up. His ears perked.

With a simple flick, Pippa tossed the rope around his neck.

He didn't like that. He pulled back, his ears flat against his head. Despite his small size, he nearly pulled her over. She planted both feet as firmly as she could on the slippery soil.

Zeph nudged the colt and gave a comforting whinny, which helped calm him down enough so Pippa could pull out the last fig.

"That's all I have," she said. "But there are more back at the stables."

The colt snorted again. He must have been in pain. Yet his enormous eyes, framed in long lashes, showed a sense of curiosity, just like his father.

Pippa held the rope carefully as she climbed on Zeph's back. "Come on," she said to him gently.

Of course, the colt was not used to people, and the temple had just collapsed around him. . . .

But she would look after him. He was Zeph's colt, after all. She promised—promised the sky, and the gods and goddesses, and the colt himself. She knew just what to name him. "*Tazo*," she whispered. It meant *to promise*.

Four

The rain continued to fall as, together, Pippa, Zeph, and Tazo began the long walk back home.

The smell of salt hung heavy in the air. It reminded Pippa of the day before the race, when the rider for Poseidon, god of the seas, had been disqualified by Zeus, his brother, for cheating. Outraged, Poseidon had caused sea water to pour from the winged horse stables, washing away hay and saddlecloths alike. Bellerophon, the groom, insisted that Poseidon stop. But to no avail. At least the horses had been out grazing at the time.

Poseidon was surely behind the storm too, thought Pippa. Maybe he was mad at the mortals, or maybe it was a grudge with a god. She didn't know, but in either case, it couldn't be good. She glanced up at the sky, shielding her eyes from the rain with her hand, wondering if she could spy him—or Zeus. All she could see were the clouds, but . . . were those stars peeking through the clouds, against a dark sky? That didn't make sense. It was late but not yet nighttime.

The sight made her shiver.

That, and the fact that her hair was drenched, and her tunic too. Zeph kept stumbling on the slick ground, making it hard for her to keep her balance, especially when she turned backward to check on Tazo.

He was soaking as well, water dripping from his feathers, mane, and tail. He wasn't shivering . . . yet. But they had to hurry. He was hurt, and a hurt horse was more likely to become ill.

That worry was soon replaced by another. They were nearing the agora, and Pippa wasn't sure what to do. There was only one road through the town, and, although the market stalls would be closed up because of the storm, she still might meet someone—a lingering merchant, a homeless beggar. She didn't want anyone seeing the colt. Who knew how they would react? She wished she had a cloak or blanket to cover Tazo's wings.

First, though, they had to pass Leda's hut. And if *Leda* saw the colt, she would tell everyone. Perhaps if they cantered—galloped even—the old woman wouldn't recognize her or see Tazo's wings. But the colt was injured, and Pippa didn't want to strain him.

Just then, Pippa spotted something through the rain: an empty sack, hanging from an olive branch in Leda's garden, likely for carrying her vegetables to the market. Pippa glanced at the old woman's hut. The shutters were closed. This was her chance.

Quickly, she slipped off Zeph and tied Tazo's makeshift rope to the branch of a tree along the road. Then she hurried into the garden.

It was filled with flowering shrubs and trees heavy with almonds, apples, and figs. Herbs and vegetables—radishes and leeks, beans and cabbages—were bowed and beaten down from the storm. Pippa darted through the vegetables, grabbing the sack from the branch. She heard a noise—a creak like a door opening—and spun around, but the door and the shutters were closed. It must have been the storm. Still, she chastised herself.

How foolish, stopping and going right into the very spot she should have passed the quickest!

But now it was done. Hurrying back to the horses, she wrung out the sackcloth, even though she knew it would soon be soaked again, then draped it gently over Tazo's back, hiding his wings as best she could. He snorted and flinched, as though it was bothering his wing.

"Please, Tazo," she whispered. "It's the only way."

Tazo didn't seem to agree. His ears were back and he looked ready to bolt. But Zeph whinnied softly and nosed him. Tazo settled, though he still gave a shudder, and Pippa prayed to Aphrodite and Zeus again, this time that the cloth would stay on and that they'd make it through the town unnoticed.

Pippa untied Tazo and they kept going. This time she walked, leading the colt, Zeph following beside him. Her sandals slapped against her feet, water squishing between her toes.

The agora was quiet. No delicious smells or lyre music filled the air. No chatter or haggling. Everyone had covered their wares and hidden away. At least, almost everyone. One woman, wrapped in a cloak that hid most of her face, hurried down the street. Pippa held her breath, but the woman merely gave Pippa a nod and didn't stop. The sackcloth had worked.

At last, they reached the farm, its sign creaking in the wind: "Stables of the Seven Sisters." The name came from both the constellation and the seven daughters of Nikon and Helena. Pippa made it eight.

As Pippa passed through the open gates, the rope jerked. She glanced back. Tazo had frozen in place, except for his tail, which flicked back and forth.

"It's okay," she said. "Just a little farther and there'll be figs for you."

But Tazo refused to budge.

A moment later she knew why.

"There you are!" came Bas's voice. Pippa turned to see him, dressed in a cloak, striding along the path toward them. "You said you weren't going riding. Astrea said I shouldn't have believed you, that she'd be riding, if she could—"

He stopped. His eyes went wide as he took in the colt.

"I found him in the forest," explained Pippa.

"And you brought him here?"

"I didn't know what else to do."

"A wild colt followed *you*?!" Bas was incredulous.

He stood, mouth wide open.

"I can't just abandon him now. He's hurt, Bas. And—"

She was about to tell him about Tazo's wings, but Bas interrupted. "We have to get out of the rain. Come on."

"To your parents?" said Pippa. "I don't think we should. Bas, I've been trying to tell you something. He has—"

"No, we shouldn't tell my parents," continued Bas. "The rain, Pippa, it's cursed! It's destroying all the crops. Everyone's frantic."

"But where can we keep him while he heals?"

Pippa thought of the solution at the same time as Bas.

"The old stables!" they both exclaimed.

Bas led the way through the pasture. Tazo was reluctant to follow at first but soon became curious, sniffing and looking at everything.

Inside the old stables it was musty but dry and quiet, except for the soft *drip-drip-drip* of a leak in one corner and the whistle of wind through the window. The sweet smell of hay filled the air, although there wasn't much hay stored there now, only a few sheaves stacked on one side, hard to see in the dim light. An old wooden cistern lay upside down, and two small stalls took up the back. A long time ago, this had been Nikon's only stable, but Pippa found that hard to imagine, with the dozen horses he cared for now.

Once he was inside, Tazo seemed to like it. He shook his head, his mane showering Pippa with water droplets.

"Tazo!" she scolded, laughing.

But Bas wasn't laughing.

His mouth hung open.

"That's his name," Pippa explained.

Still Bas didn't respond. Instead, he pointed. A single silvery-gold feather had escaped from under the sackcloth and was drifting to the ground, glinting like a star in the darkness.

"Is that . . . Is he . . . ?" Bas stammered.

Pippa nodded. "That's what I was trying to tell you."

Slowly, she removed the sackcloth from Tazo's back. He liked that and shook again, his wings shimmering and rising up slightly like two slivers of moon. He gave a short, pleased snort.

"*A winged horse*," breathed Bas. "Here. But how . . . ?"

"I don't know exactly," Pippa said. "I think his mother must be one of the wild mares. Maybe something happened to her during the storm. But Tazo *is*

Zeph's son. I'm certain. I can just tell. His coloring's the same, except the gold. I didn't know what to do, other than bring him here."

"A winged horse," Bas repeated incredulously.

"Yes," said Pippa, feeling like they'd wasted enough time, with two wet and cold horses to tend to. (Although Zeph seemed to have taken care of himself by finding the sheaves of hay.) "I think one of his wings is injured. He needs to be looked after."

"Yes, yes, of course."

Pippa draped Tazo's cloth over a beam, then wrung out her hair. While Bas fetched supplies, she settled the colt into a stall.

"I told Father I found you," Bas said when he returned. "He was happy to hear it."

"You didn't say . . . ," started Pippa.

"No, of course not," replied Bas. "Just that we were taking care of Zeph."

"Good," she replied. "You can't say *anything* to them, Bas, not until we figure out what to do."

Bas nodded solemnly.

Carefully, she rubbed Tazo down—his legs, his neck, and, as gently as she could, his wings too. Bas tried to keep him still while Pippa examined Tazo's wing.

The colt's wings were even more magical in the soft light from the oil lamp than they had been in the daylight. The feathers shimmered like real gold and were soft like rose petals, despite still being a bit damp.

Pippa touched the feathers as gently as she could. "Like your father's." She glanced over at Zeph. "Except his were bigger."

Tazo's ears flicked back, as though he didn't appreciate the comparison.

There was a deep cut, but the wing itself didn't seem broken. With fingers that could never master the loom but seemed built for this, Pippa cleaned the cut and tied a band of soft cloth around it, to keep it still and clear of infection. She didn't have any salt and vinegar to clean it, or alum, ivy root, and pitch to treat it, but she would find some tomorrow. All the while, as the rain thrummed against the roof, Bas kept Tazo distracted by feeding him figs. He liked them and would've eaten them until he was sick, as Astrea did with honey cakes.

"No more," said Pippa eventually. "He needs to eat properly."

So they fixed him a supper of barley and beans and

gave him some water, but not so much it would chill him. Then Pippa turned her attention to Zeph, who was waiting patiently in the other stall eating hay. He didn't want to leave. And neither did she.

"I can sleep here tonight," she said. "I can bring Zeph to the stables in the morning, so no one is suspicious."

"But what about you?" said Bas.

"Tell them I'm sleeping in the stables, that Zeph doesn't like the storm." It wasn't the first time Pippa had slept with the horses, but it was something Helena did not approve of, something a proper young woman would never do.

"But you're wet, and you must be hungry."

"I'll be fine," replied Pippa.

Bas shook his head but knew that it was impossible to argue.

"My parents *are* distracted by the storm," Bas said slowly. "I'll bring you supper."

"Thank you," she said.

Bas shook his head again, then gazed at Tazo, who was now suddenly asleep, his energy gone as quickly as it had come, his wings moving up and down in a steady, wavelike rhythm.

"What will we do with him?" added Bas.

"I don't know," Pippa replied. And that was the truth.

Winged horses weren't supposed to be in the mortal realm. Tazo had survived this long, but if anyone else saw him, what would happen? Who knew what others would do, if they knew a real winged horse lived below the mountain? And the gods, what would *they* do? She couldn't keep him, could she? She wanted nothing more.

"I can't believe it. I really can't believe it," murmured Bas.

Neither could Pippa. She didn't feel cold or hungry or tired. Only excited and—despite the strange and frightening storm—thankful.

Even more so when Bas returned with a plate of food. Her appetite returned at the sight and smell of the grilled fish, bread and cheese, and cup of watered-down wine.

"Helena wanted you to have this too," he said, passing her a clean peplos.

Just like Helena to think about her appearance.

Still, once Bas was gone, it felt nice to change into the clean, dry clothing. And, as she ate, guilt rose in Pippa. Helena and Nikon had given her so much—a home, food, and care. She *could* try harder.

Yet, when she finally fell asleep to the lullaby of the swishing tails and the rumble of rain, like a thousand hoofbeats, her dreams weren't filled with nightmares of being tangled in yarn. They were filled with flying, on a horse with wings that lit the sky, bright as the moon.

Five

Pippa was woken, not by the storm—but by voices. Loud ones, drifting in from outside.

She jolted up from her spot on the floor beside Zeph. Zeph was already awake, his ears pricked.

Was it day or night? Light streamed in through the window, but when Pippa looked up through it, she saw that the clouds had disappeared and the sky was filled with stars, so many, so bright it seemed like they were woven together. Nyx, goddess of night, was certainly not tangled up in the storm now, and was putting on her best display.

If it was still night—or even early morning—why the voices? It sounded like half the village was gathered outside.

"My crops will be ruined!" came one.

"It's the gods. They must be mad at us," said another.

"But why?!" burst another voice, even louder. "Why are the gods so angry?"

"I told you, because of what is here. In these old stables. Show us, boy!"

This voice belonged to a woman. It seemed familiar, but Pippa couldn't identify the speaker. She didn't need to though, to feel the jolt of fear. The woman was talking about Tazo.

Tazo was awake now too, his wings slightly raised, glimmering in the dim light in the stables. His eyes shone, and his nostrils were flared wide with fright.

Pippa's hands shook as she frantically looked for something to hide him with.

But she didn't have time.

The doors flung open, letting in more starry light and the heavy smell of salt. Although Pippa had never been to the sea, she imagined this is what it smelled like.

Tazo gave a frightened snort, shying back, as the

crowd surged into the stables. Gasps and cries of surprise and shock filled the air.

Nikon stood up front, with a lantern, shaking his head in disbelief. Bas stood beside him, his face twisted in dismay.

How could he? Pippa's heart thumped with anger, but then his eyes met hers.

"I'm sorry," Bas mouthed, and he gave her such an apologetic look she knew this wasn't his doing.

It was Leda's. The crone hobbled forward, wheezing as she spoke. "A winged horse." She pointed at Tazo.

"Oh, Pippa, what have you done?" murmured Helena. Beside her, Astrea gasped.

The colt snorted and showed the whites of his eyes. His ears were flattened on his head, and his tail clamped down.

"*Shh.* It's okay. It's okay," Pippa soothed.

Pippa kept stroking and talking to him until, at last, Tazo's trembling stopped and he was quiet.

"Where did he come from? How did he get here?" came a villager's voice.

"The gods must have sent him," said another.

"No, can't you see? He's Zeph's," piped Astrea.

There was a collective murmuring. "The winged horse's colt . . . Can it be?"

"Zephyr's colt or not, it shouldn't be here." Leda's crackly voice silenced them. "Poseidon is in charge of the seas and all horses too. No wonder the salt water poured from the sky. Poseidon does not want *his* steed on mortal soil. He is punishing us for keeping it here." Leda glared at Nikon.

"I haven't seen the creature before now," Nikon cried, raising his hands in the air.

"No, perhaps not," replied Leda. Once again, she pointed accusingly at Pippa. "I saw *her* bring it back yesterday from the hills, during the storm."

Everyone stared at Pippa, and she felt her skin prickle under their gaze.

"I found him in the woods. He was hurt," Pippa explained, trying to keep her voice calm.

"And so you brought him here? And you didn't tell me?" said Nikon. He didn't seem angry, only full of astonishment. He turned to his son. "Basileus! You should have—"

"It's not Bas's fault. And the colt isn't doing any

harm . . . ," stammered Pippa.

"Harm?! He's a curse," spat Leda.

"A curse?" Pippa shook her head. "But he's just a colt. With wings. He's a gift."

"*Ha!*" Leda spat again. "Zephyr's son has the wings that he himself lost. You might see this as a gift. But I know the truth. I know a thing or two about curses."

Her fingers curled around the cloak covering her head, and she threw it back . . . to reveal gold!

Instead of the white locks of an old woman, her hair glistened in the lantern light, like Helena's finest brooch. Leda rapped it with her knuckles.

"Yes, it really is gold," she said. "Now you all know my secret. I am a descendant of the great King Midas."

Gasps and exclamations filled the old stable, as Leda went on.

"King Midas, as many of you know, had a lust for gold, so he asked the gods to grant him a golden touch. You don't ask things of the gods. You only give. But King Midas asked, and the gods granted his wish. At first, he saw it as a gift. Until he realized that *everything* he touched became gold: the food he wanted to eat, the water he wanted to drink, even his own daughter.

He begged to have the curse reversed. Luckily, the gods took pity on him and took it away." Leda paused. "Most of you know this story. But you don't know the rest. When his daughter was brought back to life, her hair was never the same. It remained gold. And her daughter's hair was gold, and her daughter's daughter. And now, mine."

"But golden hair, that's not a curse . . . ," said Helena.

"Not a curse!" Leda laughed. "You think it's a blessing to be weighed down day and night by this golden monstrosity? It has given me this hunch. This is what comes of meddling with the gods. This is why we must destroy the colt."

"*Destroy?!*" Pippa burst out.

Zeph pawed the earth, and Tazo snorted.

"Destroy?" Nikon also looked upset.

Leda softened her tone. "I meant, of course, take it to the temple. Poseidon's temple in Iolkos. The priest there will know what to do with it."

Leda didn't have to say what she was thinking. There was only one thing priests did in their temples: make sacrifices to the gods and goddesses.

"You can't!" cried Pippa.

"Hush," said Nikon. "Leda is right. The priest will

know what to do. It's a winged horse. It belongs with the gods."

"But . . . ," stammered Pippa.

"If we don't do something," said Leda, "there is no doubt more ill fortune will rage across our lands. Poseidon's anger knows no bounds. We have to take the colt to the temple—immediately!"

Right now? Pippa's stomach tightened.

Nikon nodded. "It is the gods' horse, not a mortal one, and Leda is right. If we don't take it to the temple, who knows what further disasters might befall us."

The villagers and farmers nodded and murmured their assent.

"Bas, make sure the colt is fed," ordered Nikon. "Hippolyta, prepare Zephyr. You will be coming with us."

"Can I . . . ," started Astrea.

Helena tugged her hand. "No, *we* are going back to the oikos."

"Yes," said Nikon. "Back to my courtyard. There is much to arrange."

"And breakfast to be eaten," added Helena. "No point leaving with empty stomachs."

* * *

"I'm so sorry, Pippa," Bas babbled, as he and Pippa led the horses toward the main stables. "It's not my fault. Leda woke us up. She forced me to tell."

"It's okay," said Pippa. Though of course, it wasn't. Not at all.

The crowd had already made its way across the field to the house, disappearing from sight into the courtyard. Only Astrea lingered, watching them from afar.

"You never know what the priestess might say," Bas went on. "Perhaps we *will* be able to keep him."

Pippa shook her head. "No, Bas. You know what will happen to him. I can't do it. Zeph would never forgive me. I could never forgive myself. I have to . . ."

The plan formed as she whispered it, as they stepped inside the cool, dry stables. Her voice echoed. "I have to take Tazo to the gods myself. To the winged horse stables on Mount Olympus."

Bas shuddered. Pippa knew that, unlike her, he had no good memories of the mountain. "But we were banished. You can't go back. Who knows what Zeus will do to you! Or to Zeph!"

"I won't take Zeph, I'll go on foot." Pippa took a deep breath. "I'll explain to Zeus and Poseidon why

Tazo was here. Then I'll come home."

"You're going to talk to Zeus?" Bas shook his head in disbelief. "Pippa, you're crazy!"

"I'm going to fix things, Bas. And I'm going to save Tazo too."

The colt, as if he understood, nickered beside her.

Bas shook his head again. "You can't do this, Pippa—"

"I have to!"

"—alone," finished Bas.

Pippa's eyes widened.

"I'll come with you. We can take one of my father's horses. It will be quicker."

Pippa knew how hard it was for him to suggest this, and her heart warmed.

"It's my fault everyone saw Tazo," he continued. "I should have said no to Leda. I don't know how, but I should have."

"Oh, Bas." Pippa took a deep breath. "You can't come with me. Tazo is my responsibility. I promise, I won't be gone long. Just . . . just delay your father from coming after me. And take care of Zeph. Please."

"But . . ."

"*Please.*"

Slowly, Bas nodded. "For you, Pippa."

While Bas found a sheepskin to hide Tazo's wings, Pippa held Zeph's nose in her hands and gave him a kiss. "I won't be gone long. I promise. I'll keep your feather close."

Zeph flicked his ears, his dark eyes gazing deep into hers, full of understanding. Tazo gave a little snort.

She didn't have time to collect more than a pocketful of figs and one other thing.

Her map. The map of Mount Olympus had been a gift from the Fates, woven of their magic threads. After the race, Pippa had tried to give it to Aphrodite to return for her, but the goddess insisted that Pippa might need it one day. Had Aphrodite known about *this* day?

Pippa took the map from its hiding space in Zeph's stall and tucked it into her peplos.

There was no time to change into more suitable clothes. Besides, she couldn't go into the house to get her chiton anyway, not without raising suspicion. So she ripped her peplos along the side. At least she could run now.

When she returned, she'd never rip her dresses. She'd do everything to become a proper young woman, just as she'd promised Helena.

That was another reason she wanted to go, a reason she hadn't shared with Bas. This time on the mountain, she'd find out the facts about her parents. She'd learn exactly what happened. Then, maybe she'd finally be able to put her past to rest and focus on what she needed to learn to be a proper young woman.

"If, for some reason, the map doesn't work and you get lost, remember, just look for the stars," Bas said. "The Pleiades."

"The Seven Sisters," said Pippa; that was the constellation's other name.

"Yes. The stars shine right above here, the Stables of the Seven Sisters, so you will always know how to find your way home." Then Bas gave her his cloak, along with a hug. "You'd *better* come back," he added. "My other sisters are great and all, but you're my very favorite."

Six

The stars still filled the sky from edge to edge, but Pippa did not pause to admire them. The grass along the road, soaked and salty, licked at her legs.

She wished she could ride Tazo, but he was still young, and she doubted he would let her. He was wild and untrained. So she ran, Tazo trotting beside her, the two of them connected only by the rope. Her heart pounded with fear.

Bas would find a way to delay his father and Leda and the rest of the villagers, but not for long. And she was certain they'd be riding when they set off after her.

"Zeus, protect us," she whispered. "Keep us safe."

She thought again of Leda's story. It was true. Meddling with the gods and goddesses rarely did anyone any good. Instead, a mortal could end up turned into an echo, or a laurel tree, or perhaps a bear. She'd heard the stories. She'd lived them. She remembered the rider Theodoros, whom, it was rumored, Zeus had turned into a fish because he and his patron god, Poseidon, had cheated during training for the race.

But she also remembered how Zeus had winked at her. How they shared a deep love of winged horses. Even if Poseidon had caused the storm, it was Zeus she needed to talk to. Zeus was ruler of the gods, including his brother the god of the sea, *and* he loved horses. She was sure once she spoke with Zeus and explained everything, he would make things right.

As long as she made it to him.

As the sun slowly rose, hardly clearing the horizon, the full extent of the damage was laid bare. The storm had pounded the gardens and fields flat. Water had even flooded the houses' open courtyards and crept into some of the low-lying outbuildings. But she didn't stop to stare.

Good thing too. They had just passed the empty

town when she heard the sound of distant hooves and shouting voices.

A search party was coming after her. She and Tazo would never escape now, not on foot!

Unless . . .

She gently tugged the sheepskin off Tazo's back. If she rode him, maybe there was a chance. She was about to mount, but the bandage on his wing made her hesitate. No, she couldn't do it. Not only had he never been ridden before, but he was still injured. What if she hurt him more?

She threw the sheepskin on the ground. There was no use for it now.

"Hurry!" Pippa urged, more to herself than the colt. She ran as fast as she could into the woods, Tazo beside her.

She led Tazo through the bushes, along an old windy path that no one followed anymore. It zigzagged this way and that, but Tazo didn't seem to mind. It was a shortcut to the next town and to the mountain beyond.

The shouts grew louder. "That way! Through the bush!"

She glanced back and thought she saw Nikon

through the green and brown branches.

The undergrowth ripped Pippa's peplos and scratched at her legs. She hardly noticed.

They were going to be caught before they even had started out.

She looked for anything—a place to hide, a cave or bushes. But there was nothing. Her panic grew. Desperately she searched in her pocket for the map, not that it would be any help. It didn't detail trails so low or far from the mountain. At least, it hadn't. . . .

Her eyes went wide. There was a symbol of roses on the map that hadn't been there before!

The map had expanded to include villages and forests far beyond the great mountain, including Thessaly! And *now*, near the very spot she was standing, was a symbol of roses! Yet there were no roses on the windy trails in these woods. At least, there *hadn't* been.

But that, like the map, had changed. When she looked up, between two trees, she saw a gateway made of twisted roses.

Roses! They had marked a special trail that Aphrodite had made just for her and Bas, to lead them home from the mountain.

Was Aphrodite helping her? Or maybe the Fates?

They had given her the map, after all. And it was made from their magic threads.

She didn't really care, couldn't really think, as she ducked through the roses, pulling Tazo after her . . . and emerged at the base of Mount Olympus—grand, glorious, and capped with clouds.

She turned around, fearing Nikon and the others would follow through, but the gateway . . . was gone. The shouts and sound of hooves were gone too.

There was only the sound of birds and wind, and . . . crying?

She froze and tried to keep Tazo still. But before she had a chance to hide, a face peered around the trunk of a tree at her. A boy!

He looked puffy and pale, and his eyes were red. His dark brown hair fell like a tangled mane. He didn't look much older than her, but it was hard to tell, even when he came to stand in front of her, because he was wearing a huge cloak. It was a lion's pelt, with the head still attached. But despite its size, it looked ragged, as though it was very, very old.

"Are you okay?" Pippa asked, standing up, forgetting for a moment that Tazo was uncovered.

But the boy didn't seem to notice.

"*Okay?*" he said, rubbing his eyes. "Of course I'm okay. It's you I was worried about. You must be lost. This is the way up the mountain. It's only for us heroes to attempt."

"Heroes?" Pippa raised her eyebrows.

"Yes, heroes," said the boy. "Don't you know who I am?" He pulled himself up to his full height—which was not any taller than Pippa.

"No," replied Pippa.

The boy huffed scornfully. "Typical. I shouldn't be surprised. You *are* just a girl."

"Just a girl? Don't you know—" started Pippa, about to tell him who *she* was, that she had been one of the riders in the great Winged Horse Race. But then she remembered that proper girls weren't supposed to climb mountains, especially not on their own, when the boy interrupted.

"For your information, my name is Hero."

"Hero?"

Tazo snorted. Pippa glanced at the boy, thinking he would look at the horse and notice his wings, but he didn't.

Even though Tazo was standing right next to him and, much to Pippa's surprise, nosing his cloak. Tazo wasn't even that friendly with Bas.

Still, Hero didn't pay the horse any attention. "My name is Hero because that is exactly what I am: a hero. The great Oracle herself said so and for good reason. My ancestor was the legendary Hercules."

Hercules! Pippa had heard of him, of course. Everyone had. Hercules was a great hero who had killed the dreaded nine-headed serpent, the Hydra. He had wrestled the fearsome Cretan bull and captured the golden-horned deer of Ceryneia. And, in what was once her favorite of his deeds, he had cleaned King Augeas's stables—the largest, dirtiest stables in Greece—in a single day by redirecting a river through them. Mind you, now that Pippa had actually seen what such a flood could do, she wasn't so sure this was the best method. It just meant more cleaning.

She must have been frowning at this thought, for Hero burst out, "Oh, so you don't believe me?"

"No. I didn't say that," said Pippa taken aback.

"This proves that I am!" Hero tugged at his cloak. "This is the fur of the Nemean lion, the most fearsome lion ever known, slain by Hercules himself!" He slung the cloak back with a flourish, and it hit Tazo in the nose.

Tazo snorted again, and at last Hero noticed him. "Watch out, hors . . . ," Hero began. Then he caught sight of Tazo's wings and gulped. "A *winged* horse."

"You must be used to seeing magical animals, being a hero. Right?" Pippa prodded.

"Of . . . of course," replied Hero, though his eyes never left Tazo's wings.

"Well, my winged horse and I had better get going," said Pippa. "Good luck."

She tugged Tazo away, though Tazo seemed reluctant to come, still too interested in Hero.

"Wait!" said Hero. "Where are you going?"

"Up the mountain of course."

"Well, so am I. *I* can take you," declared Hero.

"Thank you, but I don't need your help."

Hero shook his head. "You're wrong. The gods and goddesses are mad. Didn't you see the storm? That's why I'm heading up Mount Olympus. I want to find out what's happening and make sure there are no more storms. I'm going to save everyone. You'd better come with me. I can look out for you."

"I'm fine on my own," said Pippa stoutly.

But too late. Hero had already taken the lead, with Tazo trotting happily behind. The rope in Pippa's hand grew taut, and she had no choice but to follow.

Seven

Pippa had never been very talkative. She preferred the silence of horses and the shimmer of stars at night. In her lonely life as a foundling, the constellations had been her only constant companions.

Bas was also quiet, no doubt a result of living with seven sisters.

But not Hero.

"I have always had a good sense of direction," he babbled, walking in the completely *wrong* direction. "Why, when I was only three, I walked all the way from the market to our oikos by myself."

Pippa took a different route, and Hero added, "Ah, yes, that way. I knew it was that way. I was going to suggest we turn up ahead. But we can turn now, if you'd rather."

"I'd rather," said Pippa shortly.

"I'm an excellent hunter too," Hero went on. "I trained with Orion's sword. Orion, the great hunter—the one honored in the sky as a constellation. And my father said Artemis herself, goddess of the hunt, watched over me when I was still a baby. I suppose your father brags similarly of you. It's what parents do, right?" Hero said, almost questioningly.

Pippa felt a pang. Of course she didn't know. Before she could explain, Hero went on.

"I even fought off two snakes in my cradle, just like Hercules."

"Really?" said Pippa doubtfully. "So you'll be able to catch us some supper?"

Hero paused, then laughed. "On the mountain? You can't *hunt* on the mountain. I wouldn't want to make the gods angry. Not when they already are."

"Right," said Pippa, unconvinced.

She needed to get rid of him. But what if he really did have some connection with the gods? That might help her. He did seem to have a connection to Tazo, or at least, Tazo had connected to him. Tazo was trotting right beside him. It didn't make any sense to Pippa, but sometimes you just couldn't explain the actions of horses. Except Zeph. He and Pippa understood each other so well.

She missed Zeph and touched his feather. The feather *was* longer than Tazo's, but—glancing over at the colt—surprisingly not by much.

Tazo's wings and feathers were truly remarkable. Did it have something to do with his being born of a regular and a winged horse? She wasn't sure. Although it had only been a night and a day, his wing looked like it was already healing well. His bandage had fallen off during their escape and it looked like she didn't need to replace it. Yet he still didn't seem interested in flying. She hadn't even seen him fully stretch his wings. It was as if he wasn't certain that he was a winged horse at all. He was much more interested in exploring the world on the ground.

Maybe the winged horse stables *was* the right place for him. The grooms could help him learn to use his wings. But Pippa already dreaded the day she'd have to say goodbye.

By the time night fell, after hours of Hero's jabbering, Pippa was renewed in her determination to leave him. She planned to wait until he fell asleep and then sneak off with Tazo. Unfortunately, Hero talked and talked until she fell asleep instead!

Luckily, she woke up before he did. It was early morning, and the stars once again filled the sky brighter and fuller than ever, casting a blueish light over the mountainside. Without Hero's chatter, it was silent, almost ominously so.

Tazo was sleeping and swaying unsteadily. She gave him a gentle rub on his nose, and his eyes flicked open, displeased. It took a piece of honey cake that she'd pocketed from the night before to convince him to follow her.

At last, they started out.

But they didn't get far.

They were emerging from the tree line and entering rocky meadows, when Pippa heard Hero's unmistakable voice: "Pippa! Where are you?"

Pippa scoured the area for a place to hide, and, to her luck, spotted just the thing. A humongous statue, so big it was like a mini mountain itself. It was hard to make out at first because it was so large and it had been tipped over onto its side. When Pippa tilted her head, she could see it was Poseidon, carved in marble, a giant trident in one hand and a lightning bolt in the other. There was nothing particularly strange about a giant statue of a god. Gods loved their statues! But . . . *Lightning bolts are* Zeus's *weapons.*

Pippa couldn't think on it for long though. The space between the bolt and his arm made a perfect hollow to hide, and she pulled Tazo in at once.

"Shhh," she hushed.

"Pippa?!" Hero's voice came once again, this time sounding strained. "If you're looking for breakfast, you don't need to. I brought plenty of honey cakes."

She felt bad—but only a little. This was *her* adventure. She had met this boy only yesterday.

She peeked through a crack in the marble, watching him emerge from the trees, when she noticed something that made her heart jump.

Hero wasn't the only one at the forest's edge!

There, perched in a twisted tree, was a creature she'd heard of but never seen. A creature she and Tazo must have passed under only moments before. A siren!

Half woman, half bird, sirens used their magical voices to lure humans, usually sailors, to their deaths.

But this siren was nowhere near the sea.

She sat on a bent branch, her claws curled around it tightly. Her crooked wings were the color of stormy gray waves and covered in white speckles. Her human face was partially hidden in shadows. Still, Pippa could make out enough to be terrified: a large nose, almost like a beak; a toothy mouth, open in a snore. *At least she's sleeping.*

But with the noise that Hero was making, she wouldn't be for long.

"Pippa?" he called again.

The boy looked surprisingly small, even wearing his lion's pelt.

Pippa couldn't help herself. She leaned out of the statue's hollow. "Hero! Shh!" She pointed up to the siren.

Hero didn't understand at all. Instead, he smiled, gave a big wave and shouted, *extra* loudly, "*There* you are!"

"*No . . . ,*" started Pippa.

Too late.

The siren's eyes snapped open. She opened her wings, making a whooshing sound like the crash of waves on the shore.

Hero turned.

Pippa couldn't see his reaction, but she could imagine it.

"Hero, here! Hide!" she cried.

Hero snapped his attention back to her. He didn't hesitate. He ran, tripping over his cloak, and dove into the statue's hollow, out of sight, just as the siren let out a note, the most compelling note Pippa had ever heard.

"Cover your ears!" cried Pippa.

Hero did. Tazo's ears flicked back and forth.

Pippa didn't know whether to cover her ears or the colt's. Sirens' voices didn't affect horses, did they? She didn't know. But she didn't need to decide. The siren's song was finished with just the single note. She wasn't interested in what she couldn't see. She circled in the air—once, twice—then took off, rising up into the sea of the sky.

When the siren was out of sight, Pippa breathed a sigh of relief. Hero snorted, along with Tazo, though the boy looked pale.

"What is a siren doing *here*?" Pippa murmured.

"It's because of Poseidon," said Hero in a know-it-all voice.

"But why?" said Pippa.

Hero didn't have an answer to that.

Surely *Tazo* wasn't the reason for Poseidon's ire?

"All we have to do is find Zeus," said Hero. "I bet he doesn't know what his brother is up to. I mean, he's a busy god, right? But when *I* tell him, he'll sort it out. No problem."

"But . . . ," started Pippa.

"Don't worry about the siren," said Hero, popping up his hood. "See? Now I look like a lion. Sirens aren't interested in lions. I'll keep us safe."

Pippa sighed. It seemed like she was stuck with Hero. But maybe it wasn't a bad thing, if there *were* more monsters on the mountain. She shivered. If she hadn't seen that siren . . .

She *did* feel a bit safer in numbers.

Even though, when they headed out, Hero jumped at the sight of a giant shadow . . . cast by his own cape.

Eight

I'll just ignore Hero, Pippa decided.

Luckily, that was easy to do. Meadows, dotted by small twisted trees, stretched as far as she could see. A sparkling stream wound its way between rocks like a blue ribbon. Even the air was beautiful, sweet with the perfume of wildflowers although tinged with a faint smell of salt.

Tazo was eagerly taking everything in too, darting his head this way and that.

As they continued farther up the majestic mountain and toward the stables, a tingle ran down Pippa's spine. They were truly in the realm of the gods.

Pippa looked for signs. The muses dancing, as they often did in the flowering meadows. A nymph playing in the stream, or a dryad taking care of a tree. The *aurae*, the breezes, playing a game of chase. But she couldn't see any. Not even the dangerous creatures of the mountain, like the *taraxippoi*, ghosts of children who had tried to run away from past Winged Horse Races and were now cursed to roam forever, lost on the mountain.

Still, she knew they were going the right way, for she spotted some rosebushes, though their flowers and leaves were withered. Had the salty storm poured down on the mountain as well? Why would the gods want to ruin their own home? *It's just the hot weather,* she told herself. But it wasn't very hot out. . . .

The sky had lightened, yet the sun barely peeked over the horizon, as if it were stuck there.

Strange, thought Pippa.

A crackling in a tree behind them made Pippa jump and Hero freeze. Was it a dryad at last? Or some other magical mountain being? But when Pippa spun around, all she saw was a squirrel scurrying out of view. Hero gave a nervous chuckle.

"Well, this isn't so bad," said Hero. "It's like any other mountain."

"So you haven't been here before?" asked Pippa, raising an eyebrow.

Hero puffed, continued to hike upward. "No, not exactly. But no one travels to Mount Olympus. Not even heroes."

"I've been here," said Pippa. She didn't want to sound like she was bragging, but it was about time that Hero knew.

"You have?"

Pippa nodded. "I was a rider in the last Winged Horse Race."

"You *were*?"

"Yes." Pippa smiled. For once, she filled the silence as they walked, telling him about the race and all that had happened since, even finding Tazo. Hero's eyes were wide as she told her story.

"Tazo's a lot like Zeph," finished Pippa, touching her horse's feather again in her pocket. "Except you should have seen how Zeph could fly. Tazo doesn't even seem interested."

She glanced at the colt, contentedly clopping beside

them. A butterfly fluttered past and up into the clouds. Just the sort of thing that would have enticed Zeph to swoop away. But Tazo kept clopping.

"Do you think something could be wrong with his wings?" she asked.

Hero shrugged. "He's just a colt, right? He seems fine to me. I mean, just because he's not like his father doesn't mean something's *wrong* with him." Hero adjusted his cape and added, "You know, it's a good thing that I found you. You were banished. You might need my protection."

"I don't think . . . ," started Pippa in a huff. Her words caught in her throat.

With all the talking, she hadn't realized how far they had come. Looming up in front of her were the winged horse stables!

It was easy to miss them. They were carved right into the cliffs. A facade of columns, tall and thick as the trunks of olive trees, was chiseled from the stone. The columns were two stories tall, with a long row of what looked like large windows on top for the horses to swoop in and out of.

Some of her happiest moments had been spent in

these stables caring for Zeph. At last she would see the winged horses again: Hali the ocean-blue horse, Skotos the black steed, golden Khruse. Not to mention their groom, Bellerophon.

She began to run toward the stables, when Hero called, "What's that?"

"The winged horse stables!" exclaimed Pippa. "We made it."

"No, *that*." Hero pointed to the wide steps in front that led up to the open arched entrance.

Indeed, now Pippa noticed that water was spilling down the steps and forming a stream that trickled down the mountain. Water cascaded from the stalls up top too, in a row of tiny waterfalls.

Had Poseidon flooded the stables again? But why? Where was Bellerophon? Pippa was about to call his name when she saw something floating in a puddle of water at her feet.

It was a whistle, carved from wood and shaped like a wing. *Bellerophon's* whistle!

She fished it out by its leather cord and dried it on her peplos. "This is the groom's whistle. What's it doing here?"

Hero shrugged, but his face was ashen. Even so, he

adjusted his cloak and puffed up his chest. "I am sure I can find out for you," he said, taking a step toward the stables.

"Wait," said Pippa. She hung the whistle around her neck and held it to her mouth. The whistle called winged horses. And it would surely call Bellerophon too. She blew it as hard as she could.

A high-pitched birdlike note rang through the air. Hero clapped his hands over his ears. Tazo startled and seemed to hover for a moment, the first time Pippa had seen him use his wings so well.

Pippa gazed up at the stalls, hoping to see Bellerophon emerge from the shadows. But the groom didn't appear.

Something *did* though. Some *things*. The most fearsome creatures Pippa had ever seen! Enormous serpentine fish, with heads like horses' except scaly, and long rows of teeth sharp as knives.

More monsters!

From the bottom floor, *another* water monster appeared. It had so many heads, Pippa couldn't count them. A multitude of red eyes glowered at them. Water—or maybe drool—dripped from the heads as they swayed back and forth like giant snakes.

The creature seemed to smile with all its mouths, then slithered farther out, thudding down the slippery steps toward them. When it reached dry ground, Pippa thought it would stop, but it rose up on its flippers and began to *walk* right toward them!

Pippa spun to face Hero. This monster looked similar to the Hydra that Hercules had defeated. "What should we do?" she cried. This time there was nowhere to hide.

Hero was now white as marble and shaking.

In a voice tight with panic, he yelled, *"Run!"*

Nine

Hero began to speed back down the mountainside. Pippa turned too, tugging on Tazo's rope. He had frozen, stiff and trembling.

"Come on, Tazo!" cried Pippa, tugging harder.

Then, suddenly, she didn't have to tug anymore. Tazo's legs started moving so fast they were a blur, and he was the one pulling her, his mane and tail streaming behind him.

The monster barreled after them, frighteningly fast for a creature that was meant to swim, not run. Its flippers pounded the ground. *Thud! Thud! Thud!*

It roared from all of its mouths, and its terrible breath that reeked of rotten fish blasted out, nearly making Pippa faint. She gripped a boulder to steady herself. Rocks loomed up in front of them, forming a maze. There were so many paths to choose from. Which one should they take? What if it came to a dead end?

Thud! Thud! Thud!

Pippa glanced back—and shrieked. The monster was so close now she could see thin bones of fish hanging from its teeth, and bigger bones of—what, she wasn't sure.

"This way!" came a cry.

Pippa thought it was Hero, but when she turned back, she saw an old woman gesturing from between two large boulders.

The woman was hunched and wore a cloak that shimmered like sunlight on a silver coin. The voice and the woman were familiar, yet Pippa couldn't place her. She was leaning on a carved walking stick, like that of a song-stitcher, a storyteller. Although what was a song-stitcher doing on Mount Olympus? "Come, come!" she said.

Hero didn't hesitate. Neither did Pippa. She pulled

Tazo toward the old woman, who turned and began to hobble quickly along a path between the rocks.

The sea monster roared again and bashed one of its heads against a boulder.

"Hurry!" cried the crone. For one who looked so ancient, she moved phenomenally fast.

The sea monster was still behind them, squeezing itself between the rocks. It roared a third time, and green saliva spattered her back.

"Here!" said the crone. She darted around a rock, stopping in front of another, this one particularly enormous.

"We're trapped!" cried Hero in despair, and Pippa had to agree.

"Not quite," said the woman. She pressed a smooth patch on the stone, and to Pippa's amazement, a door appeared. It swung open, and the woman disappeared within, but not before gesturing for them to follow.

Breath catching in her throat, Pippa stepped inside too, coaxing Tazo through behind her. Pippa thought he might not fit, but the doorway seemed to expand to accommodate him, and once Hero tumbled in after them, the door closed itself just as it had opened. Suddenly all was . . .

Quiet.

Pippa couldn't hear the thud or roars of the monster outside. She couldn't even see the outline of the door that they'd come through.

They were safe.

She took a deep breath and wiped the sweat from her brow. Slowly, her heartbeat returned to normal, and she looked around.

She expected it to be some sort of cave. It certainly smelled like one: musty and damp. But she was surprised to discover that it was a house.

Like most houses in Greece, all its rooms were centered around a main courtyard, except this courtyard wasn't open to the sky above but instead had a roof of stone. Still, there were plants growing along the courtyard's edge—mosses and ferns—and a small well at the back. In one corner was a stack of broken chairs, with a large, hastily made bench standing beside it. Oil lanterns set in alcoves along the wall gave out a warm, golden light. In the middle of the courtyard, there were three chairs set up, surrounding a table in the middle. On the table lay a spindle.

Two women sat beside each other, each equally as old as the woman who had brought Pippa here. Their hair was white as bones, and their faces puckered with wrinkles. One had scissors in her gnarled hand, raised as though ready to snip the air. The other was tapping a measuring stick impatiently on the table.

Pippa gasped. She knew these old ladies. She had met them before, last time on the mountain. They were Clotho, Lachesis, and Atropos, the three old women who spun, measured, and cut the threads of every mortal's life. They were almost as powerful as Zeus and equally as feared—although Aphrodite had once said, "They are merely three old ladies, and even they can only see so much."

"The Fates," Pippa whispered.

"The *Fates*?" echoed Hero.

This was confirmed a moment later when Atropos, brandishing her scissors, grumped, "Really, Clotho! The time you've wasted. The lives delayed. Did you have to go off like that?"

Clotho hurriedly hobbled to her seat and began spinning as she replied, "You heard the whistle. You knew it was time."

"Time to meddle?" said Atropos. "If it was me, I wouldn't have gone at all."

"But I brought them back, didn't I?" said Clotho,

the sweetest of the three, her spindle whirring now, as bright silvery thread was created.

"And for what?" sniffed Atropos. "The last thing we need are *more* houseguests."

Pippa wasn't sure what she meant.

But Clotho only said, "It is a shame that we don't have food to offer our guests. If only we had our garden."

Pippa remembered their garden. Zeph had liked the carrots there.

"But we had to move. We couldn't stay where we were. Not with all the disappearances," clucked Lachesis, then paused to measure a new length of thread.

"W-what disappearances?" stammered Pippa, unable to hold in her curiosity. "Why did you move here? And what about the horses? Where are they and why were the stables filled with water?"

Atropos looked up with a glare. "Humph," she said. "I knew it. Give them a moment and the questions come. Next will be 'How will I save the day?' and 'Will my name go down in the ballads like my ancestors?'" Here she shot Hero a particularly sharp scowl. "That is what you're thinking, is it not, Hero?"

"You know my name?" said Hero, sounding pleasantly surprised. "Of course, you must also know that—"

"Oh, yes, we know," said Atropos. "We know everything."

Hero's eyes went wide, and he closed his mouth.

What did they know about Hero? wondered Pippa, but only for a moment. For now, there was only one thing on her mind. "I just want to know about the horses," she said.

"Sisters," said Clotho gently, "we must tell them."

"Perhaps about the past, but not the future," reminded Lachesis.

"Of course," said Clotho.

Atropos grunted. "Not everything either. Just what *he* knows. That's only fair."

Pippa wasn't sure who "he" was, but she wanted to hear any part of the story, even if it wasn't everything. "Please, tell us," she said.

"Yes," said Clotho. "You'll want to take a seat. This is a long tale."

Pippa did so, cross-legged on the stone floor. She let go of Tazo's rope, and the colt wandered to the side of the courtyard and happily began to munch on the plants there. The Fates didn't appear to mind. Hero sat close to Pippa. She could see he was still nervous, tugging at his cloak.

As Clotho spoke, she spun her thread, thin as spider's silk but bright as gold, while Lachesis measured and Atropos snipped.

"It happened only days ago, though it seems like much longer now," she began. "On the day Athena took Zeus's throne, in reward for winning the Winged Horse Race."

"Shouldn't she have received the award long ago?" interrupted Pippa. "The race was more than two years ago."

"Time passes differently here, child," said Clotho. "The gods and goddesses live forever. Two years is nothing to them."

"Not like for you mortals," added Lachesis.

Clotho continued. "Athena, being the wise goddess she is, had nothing dramatic planned for her day as queen of the Gods. She simply wanted peace and to explore Zeus's great library. But Poseidon had other plans."

So it *had* been Poseidon! Questions swirled in Pippa's mind, but she waited for Clotho to go on.

"He used Zeus's absence to attack the gods' palace, surrounding it with sea monsters. When Zeus realized what was going on, he rushed to his winged steed, Ajax, hoping to fly up through the roof and cast his lightning bolts down upon them. But in the stables, Ajax was gone. Meanwhile, Poseidon cursed salt water to stream from above."

"So that was the cause of the storm," said Hero.

I knew it. Tazo had nothing to do with it, thought Pippa. It really hadn't been to punish mortals after all. Still, Pippa couldn't celebrate this news. "But what about Khruse, or any of the other winged horses? Couldn't Zeus have ridden one of them?" she asked.

Clotho shook her head. "Not only was Ajax gone, *all* the winged horses were."

"All?!" burst Pippa.

Atropos jumped. *Snip!*

"Oops!" she said. She held up a thread—a very long one.

"Wonderful," she griped. "Double the lifetime."

"Sorry," said Pippa, then turned back to Clotho. "Are you sure? *All* the horses are gone?"

"Yes," confirmed Clotho. "Including Helios's steeds that pull the sun across the sky, and the immortal steeds of the dawn goddess, Eos. Even the Amenoi, the gods of the four winds, who can transform into horses, can't be found. Only Poseidon's hippocampi, half horse half fish, remain."

So those were the strange creatures in the winged horse stables, thought Pippa. *Hippocampi! And Poseidon's sea monsters too. . . .*

"But he's *Zeus!*" said Hero. "Couldn't he just transform himself into a winged horse?

Clotho nodded. "Yes, but his winged horses and his lightning bolts give him extra power that the others do not have. In the stables, Zeus was attacked again. His lightning bolts were stolen from him. Not to mention his bluster . . ." She smiled wryly. "Without those things, he is no more or less formidable than any of the gods and goddesses."

Clotho went on. "No one knows where the other gods and goddesses are now. . . . But one thing is certain. The mountain is in chaos."

"But *why?*" asked Hero. "Why would Poseidon do this?"

"He was banned from the last race. He forced his rider to cheat, and so Zeus disqualified him. He was furious," said Pippa, remembering. But even as she said it, she knew it wasn't enough. Not a reason to attack all your brothers and sisters.

"Ah," said Clotho. "Yes, he was mad. But it is more than that. Poseidon has always been jealous of Zeus. Zeus, Poseidon, and Hades are brothers, you know. In fact, Poseidon is older than Zeus. It was only chance that Zeus was chosen as king."

"Chance? Pah! *Chance?!*" came a booming voice from a room to the left. "I was the one who saved all my brothers and sisters from my father's vengeful stomach! When Cronus swallowed them, it was I who freed them. I deserve my place on the throne!"

There was a whooshing sound.

"Duck!" cried Hero, pushing down Pippa's head.

Just in time! A large stick, wavy like a lightning bolt, zipped through the air and crashed into the wall, snapping in two. Tazo froze.

Atropos stood up, with a fierce snip of her shears. "What *have* I told you about throwing lightning bolts indoors, Zeus!"

Zeus?!

Ten

Zeus, king of the Gods, god of the sky, stood in the doorway, his frizzy white beard so big it nearly touched either side. He had a large bandage wrapped around his left arm and was leaning on a crutch. His flowing robes were crinkled, but the pattern of clouds and lightning bolts still shone in the lamplight. A silvery winged horse feather peeked out from his pocket, just as Pippa remembered. The god looked indomitable, but also humbler than when she'd seen him last, after the race.

Especially when he mumbled, "I'm sorry," to Atropos,

adding, "It's not like it's a real lightning bolt anyway. It's just made of wood."

"Wood or not, there's no throwing inside," Atropos scolded.

"If I had my *real* lightning bolts . . . ," he huffed.

He slumped down on the oversize bench. But when he spied Tazo by the opposite wall, he sprang up again. Tazo was still frozen, his ears pressed back and his nostrils flared.

"A horse!" Zeus exclaimed. "A winged horse! Can it be true? Have the horses been found?"

"No," said Clotho. "Only this one. They brought it." She gestured to Pippa and Hero.

Hero did not bring Tazo, Pippa wanted to say, but she didn't dare contradict a Fate, nor speak at all while face-to-face with the most powerful god on Mount Olympus.

Zeus tugged his beard, staring intently at Pippa. "You. I know you. You were the child from the race. I exiled you back to the mortal realm with your horse." He gave a half smile. "That horse was small, but what spirit."

Slowly, Pippa nodded, pleased that he had remembered Zeph, but she was still cautious. "Yes, I'm

Hippolyta," she said. Would he punish her for disobeying him?

But Zeus didn't seem to care. Instead, he pointed to Tazo. "This isn't the horse I banished."

"No," she said. "But it is his colt. I found him only a few days ago, in the wild. I didn't know what to do with him, so I brought him here."

"*We* brought him," inserted Hero.

Pippa shot him a withering glance, and Hero quickly shut his mouth.

"A colt," said Zeus slowly, stepping toward Tazo, who did not move. "Yes, he is small. But there is something about him. He looks strong. How well does he fly?"

"He doesn't," said Hero.

"Doesn't fly?" exclaimed Zeus.

"Well, not yet," hurried Hero. "Not that I've seen. I mean, he did *sort of* fly. When we were escaping the sea monster, but . . ."

"Useless!" Zeus gave a great sigh and stepped back, slumping once more onto the bench. He tugged at his beard so hard Pippa thought he might rip it out.

"How am I supposed to regain the throne? How will I defeat Poseidon without a horse and like this?"

he roared, throwing his crutch to the ground with a deafening clatter.

"But surely you and the other gods and goddesses can fight Poseidon?" said Hero. "They can help, right?"

Zeus shook his head. *"Help?* That useless bunch. Pah! When I couldn't find Ajax, I whistled for *any* horse, but none came. Instead, my whistles brought the other gods and goddesses, who also couldn't find their horses, and arrived to pester *me* about it. Not the wisest plan. As soon as we were gathered, a darkness descended—unlike any even I've seen. When the light returned, none of us had our relics, and we were sur-rounded by sea monsters, and my brother . . ."

"Sea monsters?" Hero winced.

"Everyone was captured," finished Zeus.

"But what about you? How did you escape?" asked Pippa.

Zeus puffed up. His beard puffed up too.

"I'm *Zeus*, aren't I? I fought my way out. But the oth-ers . . ." He shook his head. Zeus stood up and began to pace, limping, in a circle. "It doesn't make sense. Poseidon has never been so powerful before. How could he have gotten all our relics? How did he cast such complete darkness? Why, usually he can barely transform a man into a fish! How is it possible for him to have done all this?" He tugged at his beard again. "Bah! What does it matter! All that matters now is defeating him and punishing him for what he's done." Zeus turned to the Fates. "You must tell me how I can do this. You must tell me the future."

Atropos clucked her tongue. "Not *this* again."

"Zeus, you know you are no different from anyone else," said Lachesis. "We cannot tell you what might be."

"I don't care what *might* be," he bellowed. "I want to know what *will* be."

"Oh dear," sighed Clotho.

Zeus opened his mouth again, as though readying a new roar, but Pippa spoke first.

"He *will* fly," Pippa said. She glanced at Tazo. "He might not be flying yet. But he *will* fly. I know it."

"Yes," said Hero. "And when he does, he will be able to carry you—"

Pippa gave Hero a sharp jab with her elbow. She didn't know that, and neither did he.

"If he was trained," hurried Hero. "But he isn't. There isn't anyone to train him."

"Except one," said Clotho.

"Shhh!" scolded Atropos.

"No meddling, no meddling," cried Lachesis, poking Clotho with her measuring stick.

Too late. The words were out. Zeus's eyes gleamed. "Yes, he *can* be trained. There is a groom. She was once a great trainer of winged horses, but I banished her"—Zeus looked reflective and tugged his beard once more—"perhaps unfairly. Her name is Melanippe. She is the centaur Chiron's daughter—he is half horse, half human. Although she is not a centaur herself, no one knows horses better than she. She now runs the stables of the fire-breathing steeds, and other horses, deep underground."

Pippa had heard of Melanippe before—at least in relation to Hippolyta, her namesake. Hippolyta was a famous Amazonian warrior, and Melanippe was her sister. But she didn't know Melanippe was also the centaur's daughter.

Zeus sighed.

"But it doesn't matter. I can't take the colt to her. If Poseidon sees me, there will be war, for certain. It's useless. If only . . ."

Zeus touched the feather in his cloak. It looked like

a shooting star, and Pippa knew it belonged to Pegasus. He loved Pegasus.

Just like she loved Zeph.

It wasn't just about regaining his throne. Zeus loved the winged horses, just like her. Zeph was a winged horse too, at least he had been one. Was he in danger, even in the mortal realm?

"I can go." The words escaped Pippa's mouth before she knew what she was saying.

Hero looked at her, surprised. So did Zeus.

Pippa nodded. "Yes, I can go."

It would be risky, but if there was any chance to help Tazo and the other winged horses, she had to. Who knew how long it would take Zeus to find a way to defeat Poseidon? Months? Years? She remembered what Clotho had said. A few years wasn't anything to the gods. But it would be to Bas and his family and all the others down the mountain. If the gods and goddesses were locked away, who would take care of the crops? Who would ensure the hearths stayed warm?

But above all, the winged horses were missing, and Pippa had to help find them.

Zeus's eyes lit up. "Yes. *You* can go. Both of you." He gazed at the broken wooden lightning bolt on the floor. "Meanwhile, I will find a way to get more lightning bolts. Hephaestus usually makes them for me, but that is impossible now that he has disappeared. Perhaps if I find the Cyclopes who help forge them . . ."

"Excuse me, Zeus, but I actually didn't bring the colt here, and really I should be going home," faltered Hero.

"Yes," said Pippa. "I can go by myself." The last thing she needed was Hero with her.

"Pah!" said Zeus. "You came together, did you not? You will need all the help you can to protect that colt—and this." He threw his cloak over Tazo's back, hiding the wings from sight.

"We don't even know where that groom lives," Hero added.

"You have our map, don't you?" said Atropos, glancing at Pippa.

Pippa gulped. She was supposed to have given it back to the Fates. Would they be mad?

"Yes, I do, thank you. It's already helped me so much with the roses and . . ."

"It's just a map," sniffed Atropos. "But it will show you the way. Look for the fire stables."

Clotho raised her eyebrows at her sister.

"Even *I* wouldn't mind going back to our regular home," the oldest-looking Fate said. "And getting rid of certain houseguests."

"Oh, Atropos, really, you must learn some manners," said Clotho. "Take care, little threads. The journey is long, but together you will . . . *ow!*"

This time Atropos had poked Clotho with her shears.

"But *you* just . . . ," started Clotho.

"Tut, tut, tut!" was all Atropos said.

"Well," said Clotho, as the stone door swung open all by itself, "I can't tell you the future, but I can certainly tell you the present, and presently there is no sea monster outside the house. Or any other kind of monsters. In case you were worrying." She looked particularly at Hero.

"*I* wasn't worrying," he said stoutly.

"But thank you," Pippa added.

And with that, Pippa, Hero, and Tazo stepped outside. The stone door swung closed behind them, then disappeared completely into the mountainside.

Eleven

Pippa opened the map and consulted it. "This way," she said.

Surprisingly, Hero followed quietly, without question.

Outside the Fates' home, only dried bits of seaweed and algae remained on the rocks, remnants of the great beast. Tazo's hooves clip-clopped on the stone as they made their way toward the fire stables.

The sky seemed close, curving above them, dim and still. Usually, the weather on Mount Olympus was always changing: winds and rainbows, storms and sunshine. But not now. It was all wrong.

Pippa's stomach twisted with worry. Zeus had said the horses were gone. Did that mean the foals too? Where had Poseidon taken them? What if they weren't just hidden . . . but worse?

And what about Bellerophon? She had grown fond of the blustering groom who had taught her so much, not only about the horses and riding but also about not giving up, about believing in herself. She hoped he was safe.

Poseidon must be really jealous of Zeus, thought Pippa. Her fingers reached for the coin in her pocket, and she gripped it tightly.

Pippa understood something about jealousy. Often she'd watched families in the agora and felt a deep ache. It was unfair; she wished she had one too. She was even jealous of Hero a little. He was clearly proud of his family. It would be nice to talk about hers. But that would mean she would need to know something about them. There hadn't been a chance to ask Zeus about her family. But later. Once she'd rescued the horses. Then he would have to answer her questions.

Although Bas's family had welcomed her in, it couldn't make up for the past. Bas's sisters had grown up with a mother to teach them how to be proper young women. They knew who they were and who they were going to be. But Pippa felt . . . lost. There was a huge chasm between who she thought she was and who she was expected to be, and no map to guide her.

Yet despite her jealousy, she'd never act on it. She was not like Poseidon.

Before long they emerged from the rocks and Hero, obviously feeling safe again, began to talk.

"Those fire stables are bound to be dangerous. No wonder Zeus wanted me to come with you." He adjusted his cloak. "Zeus must have seen this cloak and known who I am. My father says that everyone recognizes this cloak. He used to wear it himself when he was young—until he killed his own lion. You should *see* the cloak he wears now! My father is very strong and powerful. He protects everyone in the town. He's even good friends with the Oracle."

Before Pippa could comment, Hero went on. "Zeus knows I'll be able to protect us. And I bet Melanippe knows all about the winged horses and where they are. Maybe they're even hidden with her. This should be easy." He pulled out a honey cake and offered it to Pippa. "Would you like a snack?"

"Hush," said Pippa. "Look."

According to the map, they should have arrived. But she couldn't see any stables. There were no buildings nearby or caves dug into the rock cliffs that loomed up beside them. The parched meadow surrounding them was home to only a few boulders and a scattering of stunted pine.

"I don't understand," said Pippa. "The map worked fine before."

"Hush." This time it was Hero who said it. He cupped a hand around his ear. Tazo had his ears pricked, as if he was listening to something too.

Actually, Pippa *could* hear something. Thumping coming from below them.

She stared at the ground, then back up at Hero. Maybe the map was right. Maybe they *were* at the stables. Maybe the stables were right beneath them!

But where was the entrance? Pippa scoured the earth but couldn't see anything. She looked back at the map to make sure. Hero peered over her shoulder.

Yes, there was the symbol of the fire stables, and this time, it showed a crack, a zigzaggy line beside it. She touched the spot wonderingly, then looked at their surroundings again—and blinked.

Although it hadn't been there before, a huge crack

in the earth had appeared in front of them.

"Whoa!" cried Hero, rubbing his eyes.

"The mountain's magic," breathed Pippa. Or was it the magic of the map itself? No matter what the Fates said, she was pretty sure it was helping her. She was *definitely* sure of one thing though. This was the entrance, and it was growing wider and wider with every second. As it did, the thumping was joined by the sound of voices.

"I can't believe we have to work here. I miss Mount Etna. This fire river is pathetic," came a piercing whine.

"At least you don't have a bad eye," replied another voice. "This light is horrible. Doesn't she realize it's hard *enough* for me to see? How does she expect me to forge metal down here? A hundred of these harnesses—this will take us weeks! And for what? The winged horses are already trapped."

"She just doesn't want them moving at all," said the first voice. "She's so particular."

Harnesses? Winged horses? Pippa's heart pounded. She glanced at Hero.

"Maybe you're right," she whispered. "Maybe the horses *are* down here."

Soon they'd see for themselves, for the crack was

growing even bigger. She, Hero, and Tazo had to hurriedly move out of its way, so as not to slip down.

The crack grew bigger and bigger still until, at last, it stopped, leaving an entrance in the center of the earth, with a path leading down it.

Pippa, Hero, and even Tazo peered down.

Below lay an enormous, shadowy cavern lit by oil sconces hung from the walls, with, at the far end, a glowing river. It bubbled and crackled, licking at the sides of the rocks like a red tongue. Pippa could feel its heat even from up above.

But the creatures in the center of the cavern were what truly drew her attention.

Two giants!

They filled the space, their skin the color of the surrounding rock and rough-looking. Hair grew on their backs in clumps like moss. They were wearing simple loincloths and nothing else.

"Cyclopes," breathed Hero.

Of course. Although she couldn't see their faces, which were turned downward to their work, these were surely the one-eyed monsters who worked with Hephaestus, the god of metalwork, in his forge in the volcanic center of Mount Etna. They had created

Poseidon's trident and Hades's helmet of invisibility. Most important of all, they were the ones who forged Zeus's thunder and lightning. They weren't forging thunder and lightning now though. They were standing at a rock table, one with a piece of leather in his hands, the other with a hammer larger than Pippa's head. Beside them was a mountain of finished harnesses.

"I'd rather get shocked by lightning bolts than see another piece of this leather," the first complained.

"At least you don't have to work with this hammer. It's a toy," grunted the other.

"If it were up to me, I'd just let the horses fly away!"

"Hush!" said the second. "We don't want her hearing. Personally, I'd prefer no more visits from Achlys."

Achlys? Pippa hadn't heard of her.

Hero shuddered. "That's the goddess of misery," he whispered. "She must be working with Poseidon. Pippa, we've got to leave."

Pippa shook her head. She peered at the map. "The stables are here. Farther down. We have to pass them."

"You've got to be kidding," murmured Hero. "We can't walk through the cavern. They'll see us."

"We *have* to," whispered Pippa firmly.

"There's got to be another option." Hero leaned over at the map. "Let me look . . ." He reached for it.

"No," said Pippa, pulling it back, while at the same time inadvertently bumping into Tazo.

Tazo whinnied, and his hooves slipped over the edge. He didn't fall though. His wings lifted, and for a moment he seemed to hover, but there was no time to celebrate. His hooves knocked some loose rocks down into the open. They fell with a clatter, the noise reverberating throughout the cavern.

The Cyclopes swiveled their humongous heads up.

"What's that?"

"Who's there?"

Their huge eyes blinked in unison. First at Pippa and Hero. Then at Tazo.

Their giant eyes grew even rounder.

Pippa staggered back, pulling Tazo.

"You! Stop!" came the giants' dreadful roar.

"Now look what you've done!" cried Hero.

"Me?" exclaimed Pippa.

But there was no time to argue. The Cyclopes lurched toward the hole, their enormous eyes blazing. One, two, three strides and they were there, hairier, smellier, bigger than Pippa could ever imagine.

Pippa stumbled, tugging at Tazo . . . his wings lifted, knocking the map out of her hand.

It rolled up with a bounce, and as it did, the ground seemed to roll up too, the entrance becoming smaller and smaller.

"HEY! STOP THAT!" cried the Cyclopes. He raised his huge hammer over his head and launched it through the shrinking entrance.

"Duck!" said Hero, falling to the ground. Pippa did, just in time. The hammer whistled over her head and crashed into a tree behind her.

She turned back to the hole—only as big as a giant's head now. . . .

There was a yell from below. "What a pathetic scrap of metal."

A massive, hairy hand reached through the hole, grasping for them, but the rocks continued closing around it, forcing it to pull back.

And then another yell, echoing off the walls of the cavern. "Stupid mortals! What do you think you're trying to do? You're going to get yourselves killed!"

"Killed . . . killed . . . killed . . ."

Twelve

Even with the entrance gone, Pippa trembled. Hero's face was pale. He lay flat on the ground and he wasn't moving.

"Are you okay?" Pippa asked.

Hero picked himself up. "H-Hercules would never have let himself get into this situation! We—we . . . should have left when I said so."

He was okay. Just scared, like her.

"They were terrifying, weren't they?" said Pippa gently. "Thank the Fates that—"

"I'm not *scared*," huffed Hero, "just surprised. And

there's no use thanking the Fates. They don't help. Didn't you hear Zeus? Besides, if the Fates helped, then I wouldn't . . ." He paused. His cheeks turned red.

"Wouldn't what?" asked Pippa.

"Never mind," Hero said. "Well, now we know what to do. It's time to go back. We'd better tell Zeus that it's impossible."

"Go back?" Pippa shook her head. "Surely there's another way in. A rear entrance that we could sneak through or . . ."

"That will probably be guarded too," Hero said as Pippa scanned the map.

She couldn't see one anyway, but the map had been changing this whole time, so maybe it would again.

"Yes, I knew it." She pointed to an imaginary spot. "There *is* a rear entrance."

"Where . . . ," started Hero, peering over her shoulder.

Pippa quickly rolled it up. "Just follow me."

Maybe she shouldn't lie to him, but he was keeping secrets from her.

Hero didn't seem to notice. "If only we knew if it was guarded or not. You know, Hercules wasn't surprised with *his* tasks. I bet he wouldn't have faced those

Cyclopes, at least not without a plan."

Hero gave a big sniff, then looked over at the colt. "I was right, what I said to Zeus. Tazo is pretty much flying," he went on proudly.

"Hovering," corrected Pippa, though she was proud of Tazo too. Still, she couldn't help thinking of Zeph and how once he could *really* fly. It would be much easier to find the fire stables if she could soar on his back now.

"Well, it was amazing," Hero said, patting Tazo on his nose. Tazo gave a funny snort that sounded like a purr.

"He does that when he's happy," noted Hero.

As Hero jabbered on—his spirits clearly revived—Pippa stopped listening, glancing back again at the map, hoping to see something new. Nothing. She sighed and stuck it in her pocket.

How did the map work? It was a secret that rested with the Fates. And what about Hero's secrets? What was he hiding from her? *I'm so tired of secrets and mysteries*, she thought as she rubbed her coin, wondering for the thousandth time about her parents. If her parents were alive, how different would her life be? Would she be in a courtyard now, helping her mother prepare food instead of escaping from one-eyed monsters on an impossible quest?

What were the Cyclopes doing with those harnesses? Maybe they *were* keeping the horses underground, all locked up. The thought of winged horses under dirt and darkness made her heart ache.

It was more important than ever to find a way in. But which way to go? The sight of something gold, shimmering in the distance beckoned her. *Maybe it's a sign*, she thought. She led them toward it.

As they marched on, Pippa took heart.

It *did* feel magical this way.

The rocks, instead of gray, were black and shimmery, slippery even. White-gold feathers were scattered here and there, so bright they were like slivers of sunbeams stuck in the rocks. Amber-weeping black poplar trees lined the way, along with a tree she had never seen before that smelled sweet, honey-like and earthy.

The golden object she'd seen at a distance was becoming clearer. It looked like an archway, sticking up from behind a black rock.

"Is that it?" asked Hero.

Pippa nodded, quickening her pace.

But it wasn't.

It was a chariot. At least part of one. A wheel hub of what once was surely the most beautiful chariot in the world, made of gold and decorated in gems. There lay a spoke, there a piece of the carriage. There the harness, with patterns of gorgeous gems and chrysolites, gleaming like tiny suns. Feathers lay scattered across the pieces like a shroud.

Everything glittered, except . . . Pippa blinked.

Suspended from one broken spoke was something strange. A dark hole, hanging in the middle of the air. Pippa reached for it, her fingers trembling. When she touched it, her fingers disappeared into darkness too, as though the thing had eaten them. She quickly pulled back. Her skin tingled.

What was it? Was it a clue to who had done this? Before she could ask him what he thought, Hero waved his hand across the broken chariot.

"This isn't an entrance," he said. "This belongs to a god. This is—this *was*—Helios's chariot. His *sun* chariot." Hero's voice wavered.

"But then how is Helios drawing the sun into the sky every morning?" wondered Pippa aloud. Even as she asked this, however, she remembered that the sun hadn't been rising to its full height, only just reaching the horizon. Maybe that was why. Helios *was* having problems.

"Pippa, show me the map," Hero went on. "Where are we? Where's the entrance?"

"Actually . . . ," started Pippa.

"There *isn't* a back entrance, is there?" Hero's eyes narrowed. "You were lying to me, weren't you? I can't believe it!"

Tazo snorted. He was frightened by the feathers, and she couldn't blame him. "It's okay," she soothed.

"It's not okay! Stop saying that!" pouted Hero. He stamped his foot.

STOMP!

Suddenly, the ground fell away. A secret door opened up below them.

And Pippa, Hero, and Tazo plunged, feetfirst, into darkness.

Thirteen

"*AHHHHHHHhhhh!!!*" Hero screamed.

Pippa's stomach lodged in her throat, and she felt like she might be sick. She couldn't see a thing.

Stone, smooth as glass, rubbed hot against her skin as she slid down what she could only imagine was a tunnel. Fast . . . faster through blackness so complete she felt like she had been swallowed by one of the Cyclopes.

There was something about darkness that made Pippa feel like she was in a place between dreams and sleep, beyond all that was real. It almost felt as if she had been there before, trapped in such impenetrable darkness. There was a voice—"I have no choice. I have to leave her"—and the sound of sobbing. Could it be . . . her mother? Were they falling into the Underworld? This wasn't how she wanted to find out her answers!

"Please, stop," she begged the voice.

A light bloomed below her—and the voice stopped, as if in answer to her plea. But instead of getting better, things grew worse.

Pippa was sliding toward a light that, as it grew bigger, grew hotter. . . . She could just make out Hero in front of her. She couldn't see the colt.

"Fire!" cried Hero. "Pippa, FIRE!"

The heat blazed upward; he was right. They were quickly nearing an opening to the tunnel. And below that lay a pool of bubbling lava.

"Stop!" shrieked Hero.

Pippa struggled to sit up and clutched frantically at the sides, but now, in the hot light, she could see the tunnel was, in fact, made of black glass and there was nothing she could grab on to except some white-gold feathers, slicked to it.

The tunnel swooped up a little, which could have slowed them enough to prevent their fall. Except they were going too fast. She looked down to see, with a gut-wrenching *whoosh*, Hero slide out over the edge.

He was gone! She slid out after him, feeling only air under her now, as she tumbled toward the pool of lava . . .

Thud!

She landed with a thump, half on top of Hero. They hadn't fallen in the lava! But then what? Where were they? She couldn't see. The heat was too much, her eyes burned and filled with tears, and she had to shield them.

Pippa felt the ground, whatever it might be, moving beneath her. Was it an earthquake?

Everything spun.

There was a jerk and a bounce. A wave of wind brushed over her, like a delicious kiss. She was moving.

She let out a long breath and, at last, opened her eyes.

She was lying in a chariot. Hero lay beside her. But was it a chariot?

Groggily, she sat up, and rubbed her eyes.

It was actually a boat. Still, like a chariot, it was being pulled by a horse attached to the yoke. The strangest, most fearsome horse she'd ever seen. Its mane and tail were made of fire! They blazed and crackled, just like the lava pool behind them. The horse lifted its head to gaze at Pippa, and its amber eyes bore into hers.

A fire horse. Could this be the fire stables?

Pippa took another deep breath and gazed around. She and Hero were in a cavern, an *enormous* cavern, with tunnels branching off in every direction. The air was filled with the smell of smoke and stone and, her favorite, the familiar smell of . . . horses.

A small group of horses, similar to the horse drawing their chariot-boat, with crimson coats and yellow-gold manes, drank from a bubbling pool of lava only a short distance away.

Other horses, these ones shining like they were wearing armor, grazed beneath metal trees hung with lustrous pearls and sparkling garnets. Beside them, Tazo was nosing a giant gem.

"Tazo!" He was there too, safe! He was okay. How had he gotten through the tunnel? He must have flown. Hearing her cry, he looked up and trotted over, his wings glittering in the jewels' light.

None of the other horses had wings except one, a creature that stood apart from the others near the center of the cavern, where a circular area was fenced off with boulders. It looked like a place to train and exercise the horses. The creature had the front of a horse, but the back feet and legs of a rooster, and an arching spray of red and orange feathers for a tail.

High above, crystals lit the cavern with a sparkling glow. And on one side, half-hidden in shadow, Pippa could just make out open stalls carved into the rock.

Her attention was brought back by a sharp whinny. The fire horse did not seem to like Tazo, who was approaching.

"Tazo, no!" said Pippa, clambering out, half falling, Hero behind her.

But that was the wrong thing to do! The chariot-boat jostled as she stumbled out of it. The fire horse turned its head and whinnied—letting out a burst of fire. The flame shot toward Pippa.

"*Stamata!*" A cry cut through the cavern, sharp as a whip.

The horse froze at once, as if the cry were a bucket of water drenching its fury. Even the flames of its mane seemed to die down to a smolder.

Heart still pounding, Pippa looked up to face a woman striding toward them. She could only tell it *was* a woman because of her auburn hair, coarse as a horse's tail, that fell all the way to the ground. Otherwise, she was dressed as a man, in a short tunic. Her face was narrow and long, with wide nostrils, and her eyes were as round and glossy as a foal's. Around her neck hung a coin, the same size and sheen as Pippa's.

Was this . . . Could this be . . . *her mother?*

The woman began to speak, but her voice was a series of snorts and clicks. Pippa didn't know what to say. Before she had to say anything though, the woman coughed. "My apologies. Sometimes I forget the language of humans. I am Melanippe, groom of these stables. Although you may call me Euippe."

Of course.

Melanippe. The fire stables. They *had* made it.

Fourteen

Euippe untied the fire horse from the chariot. The horse tossed its head, its mane spitting and crackling, then trotted off to join the other fire steeds nearby. "He does not like swimming in the lava, but it was the only way to save you. You are lucky I heard your shouts in time. Sliding down these tunnels . . ." She clicked her tongue. "Only mortals would be so foolhardy. Who are you?"

"I am Pippa and this is . . ."

"Hero, of the family of Hercules."

"Ah," Euippe's nostrils flared even wider. "You look familiar."

Hero puffed up, but only for a moment, because Euippe's gaze wasn't focused on him but on Pippa.

"I was in the race," said Pippa. "The Winged Horse Race."

This didn't seem to satisfy Euippe, but she tossed her head and continued, "Welcome to the fire stables. Your horse will be safe here. I assume you have been sent by Zeus."

"How . . . How did you . . . ?"

Melanippe shrugged off Hero's question. "Although I do not care much for the gods, I do care for the horses, and I am happy to help you. Helios's winged steeds used to stable here, but the night of the storm, they disappeared. We must bring the winged horses back."

"You know *why* we've come?" asked Pippa. "Did Zeus send you a message?"

Euippe shook her head, giving a little grunt. "Zeus sent me no message, but I know." She looked at Tazo and clicked her tongue. Then turned back to them. "You are here to train your colt, yes? But enough questions. Come. Out of that boat. Tazo is hungry, as I am sure you are too. I can set up his stall after we eat."

As Euippe led them down one of the many tunnels, which were lit by orange crystals, Hero whispered to Pippa, "We didn't tell her Tazo's name."

"We didn't tell her anything!" Pippa whispered back. "She spoke with Tazo. She must have."

"Impossible," huffed Hero under his breath.

"Anything is possible," Pippa replied. After all, they'd just seen a fire-breathing horse, hadn't they?

She glanced at Euippe with wonderment—and envy. To be able to actually speak with the horses—she would do anything to have that ability. Although a horse could tell her a lot of things, if she watched it properly. The tiny movements of its ears and eyes, its little whinnies and nickers. Pippa knew that language. So maybe she wasn't so different from the groom?

The room Euippe led them to reminded Pippa of the tack room in the winged horse stables—at first. Bridles and saddlecloths hung from hooks along the walls, and there were buckets and barrels of food. However, the halters were plated with gold and the saddlecloths made with silver thread. Instead of oats and apples filling the buckets, there were plump pomegranates and even a barrel of olive oil. Was that for the metal horses? Singed stalks of fennel hung from the ceiling.

In the center of the cave, a small table was set up. There, Euippe served Tazo a bucket of barley mash. Then she ladled some into bowls for herself, Pippa, and Hero. Pippa took a few mouthfuls to ease her growling stomach, but Hero didn't touch his. Pippa couldn't blame him. Even though she had eaten such food before, when she had no home, now she was used to the plump olives, fresh bread, and fish that Helena served.

"What do the fire horses eat?" Pippa asked.

Euippe frowned as if annoyed to be interrupted during her meal. "The same as most, with the addition of flames and meat."

"And the metal horses?"

"The metal horses—automatons—do not eat at all. Your questions tell me *you* are finished. I shall show you to your beds and Tazo to his stall."

Pippa did not like to be separated from Tazo, but she trusted Euippe because he did, and she followed her once more, this time to a set of small caves with hammocks hung between huge crystals.

"We will begin training in the morning," said Euippe.

"Do you think . . . Do you think he will really fly?" asked Pippa.

Euippe laughed. "Of course he will. He has flown already."

"You mean down from the tunnel?" asked Pippa.

Euippe gave a short nod. "There he glided, but he has flown already in the wild. Whether he will fly with a rider is another question."

Tazo had flown in the wild? Pippa could hardly believe it. But Euippe didn't say anything else. She strode down the hall, leading Tazo, her hair trailing after her. So much for asking Euippe questions. She was clearly not much of a talker.

Unlike Hero. He lingered in the hallway, even when Euippe was gone. He was a mess. Dirt and ash covered his face and cloak, and his hair was matted with sweat. Pippa imagined she looked the same.

"Do you think she can really speak with horses?" he asked. "Do you think she will help us?"

"Yes," said Pippa.

"We'll have to ask her more questions tomorrow. I can do it. I think she didn't like the questions you asked, but *I* know how to ask questions."

"You *are* good at talking," said Pippa.

Hero didn't take the hint. "I don't think Hercules ever visited the fire stables. My father, he won't believe that I'm here." Hero was still talking, even as he headed across to his room. "Pippa?"

"Yes?"

"Good night."

Pippa rolled her eyes. "Good night, Hero," she said with a smile.

Surprisingly, it *was* a good night. Despite the swaying bed and her swirling mind, Pippa slept deeply and dreamlessly.

She might have continued to sleep had someone not shaken her awake.

"*Hero,*" she grumbled, reluctantly opening her eyes.

But it wasn't Hero. And it wasn't Euippe either.

Pippa's eyes went wide in wonderment. "Sophia!" she gasped. She barely recognized the young woman in front of her, with her hair piled on her head and her lips shimmering in olive-oil mixed with beeswax.

Two years had passed, but Sophia looked much older, as though she had purposefully aged herself—which was possible, considering she was now a demigoddess. Her fingers were ink-stained, evidence she must have been reading manuscripts or writing them. Pippa could barely read, much less write. No one had ever taught her. Sophia, on the other hand, had been raised like a boy by her father and taught by scholars.

"Pippa!" Sophia exclaimed. "I heard from Euippe you were here. I wasn't sure if it really was you, but . . . oh, Pippa, how glad I am to see you!"

Sophia threw her arms around her, and Pippa almost toppled out of the hammock.

"What are you doing here?" both girls burst out at the same time, then laughed.

Sophia explained first. "Athena assigned me a task. I am writing a scroll."

"A scroll?" exclaimed Pippa, climbing out of the hammock.

"Yes, on the horses of Olympus," said Sophia proudly. "I'm focusing mostly on winged horses, but I'm including sections on the fire-breathing steeds and the automatons. Did you know that not all of them are immortal? Only some of the winged horses are. Like the Amenoi, the gods of the four winds. I was about to visit them, when Poseidon attacked. Now I dare not go anywhere. Euippe says it's not safe. Not until peace is restored between the gods and goddesses. But I don't know how that will happen, not with all the horses gone. Not to mention the gods and goddesses missing."

"That's why I'm here," said Pippa, quickly explaining everything—including that Tazo was Zeph's colt.

Sophia's eyes went wide.

"I've never heard of such a creature—part winged and part earthly horse. I'll have to include him in my writing! And Zeus is hoping to ride him?"

"Yes," said Pippa. "But he needs to be trained. That's why we're here, to get Euippe's help."

"If anyone can help, it's her," said Sophia. She lowered her voice as she confided, "Euippe wasn't always a human. For a while, she was transformed into a horse by Zeus, as punishment. Zeus eventually transformed her back and made her groom of these stables. She isn't allowed to leave."

"A horse?!" exclaimed Pippa. Now it made sense why she looked so much like one, and why Zeus had been slightly hesitant to recommend her.

Sophia nodded. "You should hear her curse Zeus. I've met lots of gods and goddesses, and Euippe is the only one who truly doesn't care what others think. Even *Athena* acknowledges that Euippe's the best at what she does. If someone challenged her to a contest of wits, she wouldn't be able to refuse. But Euippe cares only about the horses."

"Why was she cursed?" asked Pippa.

"I don't know. I've tried to ask her, but she won't say. She's not very talkative," sighed Sophia.

"I've noticed," said Pippa. "That's certainly not Hero's problem," she added in a grumble.

"Hero?"

"The boy who's with me. He says he's the descendant of Hercules, but I'm not sure. He says a lot of things that I don't think are true. Remember what you said once, that boys have the wits of a squid? I think this one would be better off *as* a squid!"

Sophia laughed.

Pippa heard a noise behind her. She turned to see Hero in the doorway, a deep frown on his face.

"Hero?" said Pippa, feeling a blush spread across her cheeks. "This is my friend Sophia."

He didn't reply, only nodded.

"Why . . . why are you here?" Pippa asked.

"Euippe called us to the training paddock."

"I can take us," said Sophia.

But Hero turned away. "I will find it myself. I have a very good sense of direction. It sounds like you two have lots you want to talk about."

Pippa watched him walk away. She shouldn't feel

badly . . . he was so annoying!

Still, she whispered to Sophia, "How much do you think he heard?"

"Don't worry about it," said Sophia. "There are more important things to think about. Like the horses." She took Pippa's hand. "Oh, Pippa, I'm so glad you're here."

Pippa smiled.

Despite everything that was going wrong, it felt right to be on Mount Olympus with a friend, about to train a winged horse.

Fifteen

As they made their way to the cavern, Sophia continued to talk, but Pippa's thoughts drifted to Hero. *It's not my fault he's here. He followed me to begin with.*

But when they reached their destination, the first thing she did was look for him. He wasn't there. Her stomach twisted.

"Don't worry," said Sophia, reading her mind. "There's more than one way to get here. Besides, it's the biggest cave of all. It's easy to find."

The cavern was even more enormous than Pippa

remembered, and hot too. Bubbles rose and popped in the pool of lava. Nearby, the fire horses were licking some rocks and the metal horses clanged as they played and galloped. In the ring in the center stood the strange half horse half rooster.

"He's a *hippalektryon*," said Sophia. "The hippalektryons were bred to be used in battle, but they weren't good at running or flying. So the breeding stopped. Now there are only a few left. Everyone views them as monsters—but actually, they're very gentle. He's the only creature at the fire stables that can fly now. Yet he's never left the caves, at least not as long as I've been here. Euippe says that he can't fly well enough."

Sophia pointed up. Pippa could just make out a sliver of light slipping through the rock ceiling, right above the pool of lava.

"There's the tunnel that leads to the surface," said Sophia.

"I know," said Pippa, with a shudder.

"It's for the most experienced winged steeds only. Helios's horses would leave from it every morning. Pippa, you should have seen them. Their wings were made of fire feathers."

"Fire feathers?"

"Feathers that can't be burned, not even by the sun. On the morning Poseidon took over the throne, they departed as usual but didn't come back. Euippe went to find out why, even though she's not supposed to leave, and when she returned, she was shaken. She said Cyclopes had taken over the entrance cavern. . . ."

"They have," said Pippa, shuddering again.

"Euippe said that a battle had taken place between all the gods and goddesses and that the winged horses have been captured."

"But where are they? Do you think she knows?"

Sophia shrugged, then shook her head. "I doubt it. She loves horses as much as you, Pippa. Euippe would do *anything* to bring them back."

Just as Sophia said her name, Euippe entered the cave, a bag slung over one shoulder. She was leading Tazo.

The colt looked wonderful. His coat was brushed and shiny, his mane and tail braided. Even his wings seemed glossier. Tazo pranced forward proudly.

"*Paue,*" commanded Euippe. Tazo stopped immediately. "Do you know the training commands?" Euippe asked Pippa.

"No, but I have this." She pulled out Bellerophon's whistle from around her neck.

"Ah." Euippe examined it. "A powerful tool. Though only good for calling horses. Not for the subtler commands. *Paue*, stop. *Petesthe*, fly up. *Basko*, speed away. You will need those to practice flying."

"You think he's ready?" asked Pippa.

"Tazo is more than ready to carry a rider. He is stronger than any young colt I have ever seen."

Sophia scribbled notes on a piece of parchment she'd drawn from her chiton.

"Although he has not learned to take a halter, he has been taught to be led," continued Euippe. "He can move according to direction, and that is enough for now. He is curious and interested in others. It is much easier to train a horse that doesn't already have a negative view of mortals . . . or gods." Euippe sniffed. "Before introducing Tazo to a saddlecloth and bridle, however, there is something else that needs to be done." She glanced around. "Where's the boy? Is he coming?"

"He's supposed to be," said Pippa.

Euippe snorted. "No matter. I need only one of you for the first part, anyway. An important part of winged horse training. All too often the grooms on Mount Olympus do not take the time to show adult horses flying with riders to the winged foals. Yet, by doing so, a foal is introduced to the concept of using its wings. Ideally, we would have other winged horses here for you or me to ride, for Tazo to be gentled. But we only have the hippalektryon Pecklion. He will have to do."

"You're going to ride the hippalektryon?" asked Pippa, surprised.

"No," said Euippe. "You are."

Now Pippa was even more surprised!

So was Sophia. "Has he ever flown with a rider? I haven't seen him do so."

"Of course he has," said Euippe. She turned to Pippa. "Come."

Pippa didn't hesitate. As surprised as she may have been, she was also excited. She hadn't ridden a winged creature since the race, before she and Zeph were banished.

Her hands shook as they made their way to the corner where Pecklion was scrabbling at the earth with one clawed foot.

Once she was close to him, she could see that he was large—larger than Tazo, easily as big as a full-grown winged horse. Unlike a winged horse, feathers didn't just cover his wings but some of his body. They were a mix of orange, red, and gold, like they had caught the colors of a sunset. His front legs had hooves while his back legs were scaly, with claws that were the color of clay.

"Pecklion is trickier to ride than a winged steed," commented Euippe. "His feathered body is slippery. And, like most hippalektryons, he refuses to be ridden with a saddlecloth. You will have to hang on to his reins very tightly."

She drew a large set of reins from her bag and handed them to Pippa, along with a handful of seeds. "This will help you put on the bridle. I will watch with Tazo and explain to him what's happening."

"You *can* talk to the horses!" Pippa exclaimed.

"Of course," Euippe huffed, but did not say more.

Pippa glanced at Sophia for help, but Sophia was still writing, clearly intent on capturing every detail.

So Pippa stepped closer to the half horse half rooster. Instead of a mane, he had a large red comb like a rooster, which stood up straight along his neck. Although his nose was a little narrower than most horses, his eyes were large and warm and reminded her of Zeph's.

He snorted and sniffed.

"Here, Pecklion, here you go." She held out her handful of seeds.

Pecklion's wet muzzle found them, and within seconds, he had munched them all up. When he was done, Pippa slipped on the bridle.

Now, for mounting. Holding the reins in one hand, she moved down to where his feathers began. Pecklion, to her relief, didn't move. Pippa tried to hoist herself onto his back, but she slipped. Blushing, she looked over at Euippe. But Euippe's face was expressionless.

Pippa tried again. This time, she made it and settled down into Pecklion's feathers. They were very soft, and she had difficulty getting a good grip with her legs. It felt like she was squeezing a pillow rather than a horse's sides.

"Up," she said. "Up." Pecklion didn't move. Then Pippa remembered Euippe's commands. "Petesthe."

With a few running steps, Pecklion flapped his wings and took off into the air. They rose up, up, up, in a jolting, unsteady manner. It was far from graceful, but still Pippa's heart lifted in joy. She was flying!

She leaned over and stroked the hippalektryon's neck. "Good job. Good, Pecklion."

Pecklion let out a squawk, and Pippa laughed. He

soared higher. It had been far too long since Pippa had done this. *This* was riding. Even if it was a bit tricky to keep her balance on the slippery feathers.

She glanced down to check that Tazo was watching. He was only a speck below, as were Euippe and Sophia.

Then Pippa saw something alarming.

Euippe was waving furiously at her. "Stop!" the groom shouted.

Pippa glanced up and suddenly realized where Pecklion was heading. Toward the ceiling and the tunnel to the surface!

But the tunnel was so narrow. He'd never make it.

"No!" Pippa said sternly. She tugged at the reins. Pecklion wouldn't turn around. Pippa pressed her legs into his sides, but it only made him jolt forward faster and angle his body until it was almost vertical.

Pippa couldn't help it. She slipped and dangled in the air. Only the reins kept her attached to Pecklion. They were stretched perfectly tight. Pippa clutched them with all her might, scrambling to find purchase on his back.

Pecklion couldn't ignore the strain. He somersaulted in the air, Pippa with him. She was sure she was going to fall. . . .

Instead, she landed on his back and desperately tried to clutch hold. The blood rushed from her head. She could hear shouts from below, and, all at once, THUMP . . .

Pecklion landed back on the ground, and Pippa slid, exhausted, onto the ground as well.

"Pippa!" cried Sophia, running over. "Are you okay?"

"Yes," she gasped, trying to catch her breath.

Euippe huffed but didn't say anything.

Someone else did, though. Hero had finally arrived. "I thought you knew how to ride," he said. "I have a very good sense of balance, just like Hercules."

Pippa scowled.

But Euippe nodded.

Pippa might not be good at cooking or weaving, but she was *great* at riding. Did Euippe really think that Hero was better than she was? Pecklion certainly seemed to think so. He had made his way to Hero and was gently nosing his cloak as if they were old friends.

"And see," said Hero. "Hercules had a way with magical animals, and I do too."

Pippa seriously doubted this. The only thing Hercules did with magical creatures was slay them! She

glanced over and thought she saw Euippe frown too—
but maybe not, because then Euippe nodded again and
said, "Hero, you will mount Tazo."

"*Tazo?* Is he really ready?" asked Pippa.

Euippe's nostrils flared. "The gentling didn't help.
We might as well move on to the next step."

"B-but . . . ," Pippa stammered. She was the one
who should ride Tazo. He was her colt!

Hero adjusted his cloak. "Hercules was very skilled
with horses. He even captured the man-eating mares
of Diomedes."

"Which didn't end well for the mares," noted
Sophia.

Pippa watched with crossed arms as Euippe placed
a saddlecloth on Tazo's back—which he was used to
for hiding his wings. This time however, it didn't cover
them. It was a special winged horse cloth that allowed
for the wings to jut out freely.

To Pippa's surprise, Tazo didn't run away when
Hero lifted himself (very ungracefully) onto his back.
Although the colt snorted and shook his head, he
stayed still! Hero's eyes widened. He too looked a little
surprised. Then he puffed up.

"Well done," said Euippe.

Pippa couldn't believe it—Hero was even able to get the colt to trot around the cave.

Still, Tazo didn't fly.

Euippe seemed frustrated. "I didn't think that the gentling frightened him, but perhaps it did," she said. She glanced at Hero. Although she didn't say it aloud, Pippa could tell she was thinking that maybe Hero should have flown on Pecklion, since the animal seemed to like him so much.

"Can't you ask the horse?" questioned Hero.

"You do not ask horses. You listen," said Euippe.

Pippa couldn't listen to Tazo the way Euippe could. She could watch though. She gazed at Tazo, trotting around the cave beside Pecklion. The stones and rubble didn't seem to bother him. He seemed to have gotten over his fear from the temple. Remembering the temple gave Pippa an idea.

"Perhaps he won't fly because of his hurt wing," said Pippa.

"He doesn't have a hurt wing," said Euippe. "I examined him closely."

"But he did," said Pippa. "He was trapped in a stone temple when I found him. His wing had a bad cut on it, and I think it might have been bruised too. I bandaged it. Maybe I didn't do a good job. I didn't leave the bandage on for long."

"No," said Euippe slowly. "You did an excellent job. I examined his wings and they are very strong, stronger than any I have seen. In fact, I am surprised to learn one of them was hurt."

She held Pippa's gaze for a long moment. "You healed this winged horse." Her eyes seemed to soften. "You really *do* remind me of someone. I wonder . . ." She let out a long breath. There was a moment of silence. Then at last she said, "Come, let's put Tazo and Pecklion in their stalls to rest. It is time for a story."

Sophia raised her eyebrows. "But, Euippe, you *never* tell stories."

Sixteen

Back at the table, surrounded by buckets and tack, Euippe scooped barley into bowls again for Pippa, Hero, and now Sophia. Pippa was too curious to eat. Euippe sat down, fiddling with her long hair. She didn't eat either.

"I haven't always been groom of these stables," she began.

Sophia pulled out her parchment and began to scribble furiously. Euippe scowled. Sophia quickly set down her stylus.

Euippe continued. "Once, I was groom of the winged

horse stables, alongside Bellerophon. I have always been good with horses. It comes of having a centaur for a father. My greatest pleasure was to train the winged horses for the race. But that wasn't all I did. The gods and goddesses do not treat injured horses kindly. If a horse has an illness or hurts a wing, even just a sprain . . ."

"The Graveyard of Wings," Pippa said in a hush. Ares had told her about it. He had threatened to send Zeph there, certain the little horse would never win the race. Pippa understood why you might kill a horse to put it out of pain. She had seen this done back in Athens. But if a horse could be healed . . .

Euippe nodded. "That's why I had another job. Under the cloak of night, I ferried hurt horses off the mountain to be cared for in secret by two mortals who owned a stable. I would leave a special token to let them know a winged horse was coming. When the horse was better, they would leave me one to bring the healed horse back."

"So there *were* winged horses below the mountains!" gasped Pippa.

Euippe nodded. "No one was the wiser. I wore a disguise. I was very careful to bring the horses down before any other gods and goddesses found out about their injuries, and when I brought the horses back up, the gods and goddesses merely thought I was returning horses that had wandered off. The arrangement worked for years, until . . ."

She paused, and all three children leaned forward in anticipation.

"Until one night—a dark, dark night—when the mortals went missing. No one picked up the injured winged horse from where I had left him. All was revealed, and I was punished by Zeus. He turned me into a horse myself."

She snorted softly and leaned away from the table.

"Oh," breathed Pippa. "But . . . but I thought Zeus loved horses. He loves Pegasus. Surely he'd want to help any that were injured?"

"Ha!" exclaimed Euippe. "Zeus *does* love horses. He was the one who made all the arrangements for them in the first place! In fact, the tokens were his too, charmed to protect the mortals. Yet the token didn't protect them. I never saw it or them again."

Now Pippa was truly confused.

So, it seemed, were Sophia and Hero.

"Then why did Zeus need to hide them? Why did he punish you?" stammered Hero.

"The gods and goddesses, especially Zeus, must always put on a show," said Euippe. "They cannot bear to look weak."

"That's why they never refuse a bet either," said Sophia.

Euippe nodded. "Zeus wanted his tender heart to be kept secret, and when his arrangements were discovered, he denied all knowledge of them. That's why he was quick to punish me. Eventually, he turned me back to myself and sent me here, to look after the horses underground. Sometimes I wish I had remained a horse. Life was simpler. Don't get me wrong. These horses mean so much to me, even the poor hippalektryon. But, like Pecklion, I miss the sun. I miss the stars. I have never even had the pleasure of watching the Winged Horse Race." She sighed.

Pippa's brow furrowed. If Euippe hadn't watched the last race, then why did she recognize Pippa? Where else could the groom have seen her? Did it have something to do with her parents? Before she could think more on this, a voice thick as syrup echoed through the cavern.

"Ah, there you are!" Everyone froze as a figure strode through the shadowy tunnel toward them.

Dressed in black robes, with two spiky wings protruding from his back, he looked like a giant bat. A bag was slung over his shoulder. For a moment, Pippa thought she saw it move. *It's just a trick of the light*, she thought. Still, she shivered.

Dark shadows circled his eyes, as if he hadn't slept in days—maybe months. Pippa wasn't surprised when he gave a great yawn. The whole room seemed to shudder from its force. Then he said, "I am Morpheus, god of dreams. I am looking for Melanippe."

Euippe stood up. "Morpheus, to what do I owe this visit?"

"Not pleasure, that's for certain," the god said. He glared at Pippa and Hero. "The stench of mortals drew me to this cave. What are they doing here?" He puzzled over Pippa's face. She hoped he hadn't been at the race either and didn't recognize her.

"I'm not an ordinary mortal. I'm descended from Hercules," started Hero. "I have completed great feats already, on this quest alone."

"Yes, the boy is a relative of Hercules," hurried Euippe. "And the girl is with him. They have their reasons for being here, as you must have yours. Tell me."

"If you must know," said Morpheus, yawning

again, "I need a horse. Can you believe that lately I've had to fly with my *own* wings to deliver my dreams and nightmares? Do you know how tiring it is? Do you know how big the mortal realm is? You'd think she would have spared me *one* winged horse."

She? wondered Pippa. Did he mean the goddess of misery? The Cyclopes had said she was working with Poseidon.

Morpheus went on. "Just *one*. I asked right away, when Poseidon was in the Underworld. But no, they didn't listen. Last night I was too tired to make my deliveries. The mortals are fearful about everything right now—their crops, the gods, their future. Do you have any idea how many opportunities I'm missing?" He patted the bag that was slung over his shoulder, and this time it definitely moved! There was something— maybe *many* things—alive in it! Another shiver ran down Pippa's spine.

"There are rumors of a winged horse. The water monsters spotted one. You don't have it here, do you?" said the god.

Pippa and Hero exchanged a worried glance.

"No," said Euippe matter-of-factly.

"There is a big reward for it if it is found," said

Morpheus. "And if it is discovered to be hidden—well, you can imagine . . ."

"We have only the fire breathers and the automatons," continued Euippe, "and a hippalektryon. I could show you them."

"Very—ahhhh—well," said the god, with another yawn.

Euippe nodded and waved to Pippa. "Go, prepare them for viewing."

"Prepare?" said Pippa, puzzled.

Euippe glared at her.

Of course! Tazo was in the cavern. If Morpheus saw Tazo he would know the winged horse was there!

"Yes, Euippe," said Pippa, leaving the room with Hero and Sophia close behind.

"So Poseidon visited the Underworld," whispered Pippa, as they rushed down the tunnel. "Maybe he was visiting someone there. Maybe . . . maybe that's where the winged horses are."

"No, because why would Morpheus be here, then?" said Sophia.

"Right . . . ," replied Pippa. Still, now Pippa knew that Poseidon had been in the Underworld. That was something. Something she could tell Zeus. Maybe even something that put her one step closer to finding the horses.

When they reached the cavern, Pippa's thoughts changed to focus on only one horse. Tazo. He was happily resting. Pecklion, in the stall beside his, seemed to be napping. All the stalls in this row had no gates, only simple ropes. Another row off to the side had metal chains for the fire horses.

There was nothing to hide a horse. Zeus's cloak, which had hidden Tazo's wings on their way to the stables, had long been lost to the fire river.

Pippa could hear voices coming down the tunnel. Euippe and Morpheus were on their way already. "I don't want to see the fire horses if they cannot fly," came Morpheus's voice. "Take me to this rooster beast."

"Think!" cried Pippa.

"There's nothing," exclaimed Sophia.

"Nothing," repeated Hero. He shook his head, and his lion-headed cloak shook along with him.

"That's it!" said Pippa. She grabbed Hero's cloak.

"Hey!" he protested.

But Pippa tugged it away from him. Unfastening the rope across the stall, she threw the cloak over Tazo's back. The lion skin covered his wings perfectly.

As Pippa adjusted the lion head over Tazo's, she was worried he might be scared, but again he seemed to understand the urgency of the situation. The lion head rested over his ears; the disguise was complete.

Just in time.

Euippe and Morpheus strode up to the stalls. If Euippe paused for even a blink of an eye at the strange sight of Tazo, it was unnoticeable.

Hero's face was red. But neither goddess nor god seemed to notice that either.

"That doesn't look like a rooster," said Morpheus, his eyes narrowing at Tazo. Pippa's heart pounded so hard, she feared Morpheus would hear it.

"Because it's not," said Euippe coolly.

"What is it?"

"An unfortunate creature," said Euippe. "Burned by lava and forced to take the skin of another."

Morpheus frowned and Pippa held her breath. But Euippe continued, "Come, let me show you Pecklion."

The hippalektryon had woken, and his eyes were fixed on Morpheus. His rooster's comb stood straight up on his head.

"*This* is the creature?" Morpheus curled his lip in disgust. "Are you sure he can fly?"

"He can fly," burst Pippa, though she regretted it at once. As much as Pecklion might want to return to the surface, he surely didn't want to go as Morpheus's mount.

"I have met rabbits far more frightful. But since there is no other choice, I will try him."

"He prefers not to wear a saddlecloth," started Euippe.

Morpheus scowled viciously—or at least tried to, before his expression turned into yet another yawn. "Very well. Ready him for me."

Euippe gestured to Hero, who looked surprised for a moment, then hurried into Pecklion's stall. He slipped on the hippalektryon's bridle and led him out. Pecklion did not want to come any closer to the god of dreams and nightmares. Hero tugged, but the creature stepped back.

"Bring him to me!" ordered Morpheus.

It wasn't just Morpheus who was impatient. The bag at his side jostled and jerked as if whatever was within wanted to get out. Morpheus pushed the bag aside, and as the bag shifted, something escaped from it.

A blur, like a black, shimmering butterfly.

It all happened so fast, Pippa didn't have a chance to stop him. *Whoosh!* Tazo tore out of his stall. Off flew Hero's cloak, crumpling to the floor. The colt's wings—golden, glorious—spread open and up, up, up he soared after the creature.

He *could* fly! He was flying! He was fast and strong and beautiful and everything she imagined. But Pippa couldn't celebrate.

"A winged horse!" exclaimed Morpheus. "You do have one here! You lied, Euippe."

Morpheus opened his sack, wide enough for a host of horselike creatures to burst out, tiny and terrifying. Their manes and tails wafted like moonlit smoke, and their bodies seemed knit from shadows.

"Nightmares!" cried Sophia. "I've only read about them."

They swarmed up to Tazo, who looked dismayed that he'd ever chased one to begin with.

"Stop!" cried Pippa.

Tazo surged forward, swerving to avoid the little beasts, heading up, up, up to the light, to the tunnel that led to the surface.

"Tazo!" yelled Pippa.

"Go!" cried Euippe. She pushed Pippa toward Pecklion. As she did, her necklace swung out, the coin turning to reveal the imprint of a winged horse— exactly like Pippa's. Euippe's eyes bore into hers.

"There is something else I wanted to tell you," she rushed, her eyes glinting. "I think that you are . . . *AIE!*"

A nightmare grabbed at Euippe's long hair. She struggled to knock it away. *"Go!"* she cried, sounding desperate now.

Pippa leaped on Pecklion's back.

"B-but . . . ," stammered Hero, reaching back toward his cloak, which lay in a heap on the ground.

Before he had a chance to seize it, Euippe snatched him up and lifted him onto the hippalektryon's back, behind Pippa. Then she gave Pecklion a firm shove with her palm, which sent him running, jumping up . . . flying!

Pippa glanced down and saw Morpheus reach into his sack—not to release another nightmare but to pull out a twisted horn. He shook the horn in the air, and a spray of silvery dust spilled out, fluttering down on Euippe and Sophia, who instantly collapsed to the ground, asleep.

Morpheus blew into the horn this time, and a bigger burst erupted up into the air. But Pecklion beat his wings at exactly the same time, and to Morpheus's surprise, the dust rained back down.

Right onto him!

He groaned and rolled his eyes. "Of all the fates!" he spat, but even he couldn't resist his own magic. He gave a yawn that rumbled the rocks and cried, "Just you wait! This isn't overrrr . . . ," before falling down with a thud, sound asleep.

"Thank Zeus!" cried Hero. "He can't follow us now."

Pippa wasn't so thankful.

"Hold on!" she cried, gathering the dangling reins. Hero gripped her neck.

Pecklion's feathers were as slippery as before, but this time Pippa was focused. She had to be. Morpheus might be sleeping, but his nightmares weren't.

The nightmares swarmed them, biting at their clothes and nipping at their skin.

"Ow! Ah!" cried Hero, clutching Pippa's neck so tightly she found it difficult to breathe.

Then, the nightmares began to shift. The one

beside her changed shape from a tiny horse to—Zeph! A little Zeph with an arrow through his chest and blood pouring out.

"*No!*" cried Pippa. Then the nightmare shifted again, this time to a bassinet with a crying baby inside. Was it her, abandoned in the darkness?

"Help!" cried Pippa.

She closed her eyes, and when she opened them, she didn't see any nightmares. They had turned back. But up ahead was something worse.

Tazo was disappearing through the tunnel of light, and Pecklion was headed there too!

But Pecklion, large and ungainly, would never make it.

Still, he angled his body, and Pippa felt herself slipping, pulled back by the weight of Hero. She closed her eyes again, heard the crack and crumble of stones falling. What was happening? She wasn't sure. She couldn't tell, couldn't breathe, even her heart seemed to have stopped. Were they flying? Or about to fall . . . ?

Seventeen

Kikirikiki!

A crow filled the air. Surprised by the sound, Pippa opened her eyes just as they landed with a lurch.

They had made it!

Pecklion was standing on the mountainside. A grassy meadow stretched out around them. The sun was low on the horizon, but even so, everything was far brighter than it had been in the caves, and Pippa blinked several times as her eyes adjusted.

To her relief, Tazo was nearby, grazing. Hero tumbled off Pecklion's back, and Pippa followed, happy to feel solid ground under her sandals.

"You did it, Pecklion!" she said to the great beast.

Pecklion crowed for a second time—proudly, joyfully—and lifted his head toward the dusky sky, as though he couldn't believe he was free of the caves at last.

But Hero looked far from joyful. His mouth was twisted, and he clutched himself tightly.

"Are you hurt?" exclaimed Pippa.

Hero gulped. "My cloak! My cloak is down there! I *need* my cloak!"

"Oh," replied Pippa, with a sigh of relief. "That's all."

"All?!" burst the boy. "It belonged to Hercules! It's the Nemean cloak! I can't lose it! My father will be furious!"

"But he gave it to you, didn't he?" said Pippa.

Hero pointed at Pippa. His finger trembled. "This is all *your* fault. You took it from me. I said no, but you didn't listen." He jabbed at her chest with his finger.

"Hey!" said Pippa. "You know there was no other choice. We had to hide Tazo."

"It didn't hide him, though, did it? And now it's gone!" He slumped down beside the tunnel.

"I'm sorry," said Pippa, thinking of how it might

feel to lose her coin. "I really am. But there's nothing we can do about it. Come on, Hero." She tried to tug him up, but he shrugged her away.

She tried another tactic. "Since we don't have anything to hide Tazo with, we better start moving. Who knows if Morpheus will sleep for long." She paused, thinking of Euippe and Sophia and hoping no harm had come to them. They *were* demigoddesses, so surely they could take care of themselves. She continued, "And who knows who else might come after us. You heard him. Everyone is looking for Tazo. We have to get back to the Fates' house. There's lots to tell Zeus. Tazo *can* fly, after all." She glanced at the colt proudly and pulled out her map.

Hero didn't budge.

"Come on," said Pippa again. "Try to forget about the cape. You were relying on it too much anyway."

"Relying on it?!" Hero jumped up. "Like you rely on that map? You never let me look at it. Zeus put me in charge of this adventure too."

He grabbed a corner of the map. The map wasn't made of parchment. It had been woven from the Fates' magic threads.

"Hey!" cried Pippa.

Hero ignored her and tugged. One hard tug. But instead of tugging it out of her hands . . .

Whish!

All at once, in the blink of an eye, the map unraveled and fell to the ground in a heap of golden, shimmering threads. Pippa's eyes grew wide in horror.

"What have you done?!" she cried. "That was a gift!"

Hero also looked horrified. But only for a moment. "My cloak was a present," he humphed. "You didn't seem to care about *that*."

"It was just a cloak! This map was *important!*" stormed Pippa. "It was from the Fates!"

"I-I . . . ," stammered Hero.

Pippa couldn't stop herself. "*You!* That's all you think about. That cloak wasn't helping you. You aren't *anything* like Hercules. The only part of you that's a hero is your name!"

Hero went pale. "At least I try to *act* like a hero. I don't whisper about people behind their backs. I'm *much* smarter than a squid," he grunted. "I know you don't want me with you. I don't care. I'm used to it. I'm better alone anyway. I'll find my way to the Fates' house without a stupid map."

"Like you found your way to the cavern?" huffed
Pippa.

"I *did* find my way to the cavern," said Hero.

"*Eventually*," said Pippa.

"Well that's good enough, isn't it?" said Hero. "I'm
done talking."

"Really? *You?*"

Hero clenched his fists. But he didn't reply. Instead,
he spun around and took a few steps away from her.

"Good! Leave!" cried Pippa.

Hero still didn't say anything. His steps grew more
purposeful, faster.

"That's fine by me!" said Pippa.

She watched as he headed down the mountain.
He looked very small and very thin without his thick
cloak. She didn't care. She turned away from him, to
face Pecklion and Tazo.

Their ears were pricked and eyes wide, as though
they had understood everything. Without warning,
Pecklion began to trot, passing Pippa, and running
down the mountain, obediently following Hero. Tazo
took a few hesitant steps as well.

"Not you too, Tazo?" Pippa whispered.

Clip-clop, clip-clop. The horse continued.

"Tazo!" she tried, louder.

She reached out to grab his mane, but his trot quickened, and she missed, stumbling on some loose stones.

She righted herself and grabbed the whistle around her neck, Bellerophon's whistle. She blew it, and the sharp sound rang through the air. But Tazo didn't turn. He hadn't been trained, like the other winged horses— like Zeph—to come at its call.

Zeph wouldn't leave her. He'd *never* leave her. But this wasn't Zeph. This was Tazo.

All she could do was watch as the colt joined Pecklion and Hero. The three of them disappeared down the mountain, leaving her alone with the shimmering remains of the map at her feet.

How *could* Hero?

She felt heat build in her stomach as if, like the fire horses, she had drunk from the pool of lava. She'd show him. She'd get to the Fates' house first, even without a map, and tell Zeus everything.

She scooped up the threads and put them in her pocket. Then she too started down the mountain, in the opposite direction.

As the sun, barely above the horizon to begin with, slipped away, Pippa thought of Euippe and Sophia.

I wish Sophia were here, thought Pippa. Sophia was a much better friend than Hero. Was Hero even a friend? Her stomach twisted. He was right about one thing; she hadn't treated him like one.

A shadow flickered by, and she jumped.

But it was just a leaf. Still, she shuddered, remembering the nightmares, and something else that haunted the mountain. The taraxippoi, the ghost children. She and Zeph had almost been captured by them while training for the race. Would the taraxippoi find her first or would Morpheus? Either way, she was lost.

She probably wouldn't make it off this mountain. She'd never see Zeph, her Zeph, again. Or any horse . . .

But just as she thought this, she saw one, shimmering under the stars, standing very, very still.

Still as stone.

That's because it *was* stone. It was a statue, atop a mound of earth. Its wings were stretched to the sky, its head poised toward the moon. It looked startlingly familiar. Where had she seen a horse like this before?

Her coin! It was exactly the same as the horse imprinted on her coin. Not just *her* coin, Euippe's too.

But why was the statue here? What was it marking?

Pippa stepped closer and peered beyond it. Plots of earth, some covered in long grass, others sunken with age, stretched out into the distance.

Pippa began to tremble. Could this be? The Graveyard of Wings. The place where winged horses—those that were not immortal—were laid to rest. This was where Euippe was trying to keep horses from ending up before their time. Was that why the groom's coin looked so much like the statue? But why was Pippa's coin the same? She didn't know. And what was it that Euippe had been trying to tell her?

One thing she did know, however: she couldn't see any fresh graves. Only the grass and a few trees, hung with shadows. The winged horses she was searching for weren't trapped here, and that gave her some relief.

But it was fleeting. She shivered. She felt cold and alone . . . and *mortal*.

When she had been part of the race, she had never cared about the prize to become a demigoddess. All she'd wanted was to keep Zeph. (Zeph . . . how she missed him!) But now she wished she *had* cared more about it. Sophia and Euippe didn't have to worry about weaving or cooking or cleaning. Sophia could work on her scroll, and Euippe cared for horses. But . . . once this was all over, Pippa would return to Bas's farm and her lessons with Helena. She would never see the winged horses again. Not that she'd ever see them anyway. They were captured . . . Tazo was gone. She felt limp like the threads in her pocket. She slumped to the ground.

And sprang up again when she heard the crunching of rocks and grass.

She inhaled sharply. Who—or what—was there?

The starlight seemed almost brighter than the sun, yet there was no warmth in it. The rocks and grasses shone silver and cold. Pippa glanced around, frightened. The noise grew louder. There was the shape of a horse, but this one was not a statue. This one was moving, shimmering in the light. Its wings were slightly lifted, and it seemed like its hooves were lifting from the ground too. A ghost!

Pippa stumbled back, away from the statue, away from the Graveyard of Wings, into the meadows. The horse followed, closer, closer . . . and let out a snorting whinny.

A whinny that sounded familiar.

It wasn't a ghost horse at all. It was . . . "Tazo!"

Pippa stopped. "Tazo!" she exclaimed again and ran to him. She threw her arms around his neck and breathed in his warm horsey smell. When she'd had her fill, she checked to see if Hero or Pecklion was with him, but they weren't. Still, *he* was there. She gave him another hug, and he replied with a purring snort. What was it that Hero had said? That was Tazo's happy noise. She smiled.

But how had Tazo found her? As though he could read her mind, he sniffed, his nostrils widening.

"It's lucky you can find your way by smell. If only I could navigate so easily. Without a map it's useless."

Tazo nuzzled her shoulder, and she rubbed his neck. "I'm glad you're back. It's all Hero's fault," she continued. This time, however, Tazo pulled away and snorted.

"I mean, really, Tazo, you can't honestly think he . . ." She bit her tongue. Tazo clearly liked Hero, and besides, what was the point of blaming Hero anymore? He hadn't meant to ruin it.

Truthfully, a bit of her missed him. At least they could have been lost together. But Tazo was with her now.

And it wasn't pitch-black. That was something.

Pippa gazed up at the stars. They filled the sky, edge to edge.

She had spent many a night when she was young staring up at the stars, at the constellation of Pegasus, wishing she could be with the winged horses. As much as she gazed at Pegasus, however, he had never led her to them. But maybe the stars *could* lead her down the mountain!

She remembered what Bas had said: the stars in the Pleiades constellation shone right above the Stables of the Seven Sisters. If she could make her way to the stables, she might not find the home of the Fates, but at least she wouldn't be lost.

She searched the sky for the cluster of seven tiny stars.

Look as she may though, she couldn't find them.

That's strange, she thought.

She tried to find Pegasus instead. Even the winged horse was impossible to spot. There were just too many stars, crowded together. Except she thought she *could* see a horse, now that she looked again. It wasn't Pegasus, but it was definitely a horse.

"Maybe Nikomedes," she reasoned. He had been Zeus's last winged steed before Ajax, and, like Pegasus, was now a constellation. But, there was another horse shape . . . and another . . .

The sky was filled with horses. One winged horse flew beside the Little Bear constellation, and another beside the Big Bear. There was a horse near Orion's belt, his nose reaching up as if to give it a nibble. So many horses, Pippa could hardly believe it.

"The winged horses!" she gasped. "Tazo, we've found them!"

Eighteen

The little horse perked his ears and looked up too.

Pippa's mind spun. Honoring Zeus's steeds by turning them into constellations was one thing. Each of those horses had worked for the great god for a hundred years, carrying his lightning bolts and flying him through storms. They were ready for rest. But it was quite another to trap a horse in the sky against its will. She remembered the harnesses the Cyclopes were constructing. Maybe they were to hold the horses in the sky?

Pippa couldn't help herself. The blood pounded in her head. "Let's fly! Let's fly to them, Tazo!" she cried.

Although she'd never ridden him before—only Hero had—she mounted easily, maybe because she didn't hesitate. His back was smooth and his mane coarse in her grasp. She held her legs by his sides, to allow room for his wings. It felt just like mounting Zeph.

They quivered, and Pippa felt quivery too. If she was closer to the stars, she might even be able to make out the Seven Sisters as well.

"Up, Tazo!" she whispered.

But Tazo didn't move.

She tried Euippe's word—"Petesthe!"—leaning forward so her chest was pressed against his neck. His wings quivered more quickly, but still he did not take flight.

"You can fly," Pippa encouraged. "I *know* you can."

Chasing after the escaped nightmare had helped him fly before. She was trying to figure out what would work instead, when, "Wait!" came a cry from above.

Pippa looked up to see Hero, on the back of Pecklion.

The hippalektryon landed with a thud, and Hero tumbled off his back.

"Hero!" Pippa cried, dismounting, surprised at how happy she was to see him.

He was trembling.

"These—these *things* found us," he stammered. "I didn't see them coming, but Tazo must have because he took off. They surrounded me and Pecklion."

"*They?*"

"I don't know what they were. None of the stories about Hercules ever mentioned them. They were children, but not quite. Ghosts, maybe."

"The taraxippoi," gasped Pippa. "You were surrounded by them and you escaped?" For once, she knew he was telling the truth and she couldn't help being impressed.

Hero began to puff up. "*I* wasn't scared. I was going to fight . . ." Then he paused and shook his head. "Actually, that's not true. I was *really* scared. I wouldn't have escaped if it hadn't been for Pecklion. He stayed by my side and I mounted him just in time. I-I hoped Tazo had found you. I'm sorry, Pippa."

Pippa nodded. "Me too."

"I didn't mean . . . I mean . . . There's something I need to tell you."

"Me too," Pippa repeated. She could hardly hold it in. "Hero, I found the horses!"

Before Hero could respond, however, a voice replied:

"And I've found you."

Pippa spun around. Morpheus! The god was standing in front of them, his horn in one hand. He looked far less sleepy than before. In fact, his eyes glinted with pleasure.

"I knew following the taraxippoi would lead me to you. They always find those who are lost." He reached a hand toward the colt. "How pleased she will be with me." He grinned.

"You can't take Tazo," cried Pippa. "You can't give him to Poseidon to turn into stars!"

"Stars?" Hero gasped.

"You figured it out," said Morpheus, in his syrupy voice. "Well, *almost.* Clever mortal. Too bad your fate has been determined. And it isn't a pleasant one."

With that, instead of shaking or blowing the horn he was holding, he put his hand in it and pulled out a fistful of dust.

Poof! He threw it at them.

Before Pippa could say anything, or *do* anything, the silvery drops, fine as mist, sprinkled over her like the tears of stars and immediately her eyes closed into darkness.

Darkness . . . so thick she could touch it. A kiss . . . The glint of a coin . . . A promise, muffled by the gurgle of a well, "I will be back." The kind of terrible, dreadful promise she knew would be broken even as it was made. Then quiet. She was hungry, cold, scared. Her heart felt as broken as the promise. She cried out, but nobody came. The darkness surrounded her, starless and stark and smothering. She couldn't breathe. . . .

Pippa woke, gasping, and sat up. She reached for the coin in her pocket to comfort her. As she traced the outline of the winged horse with her fingers, her hammering heart calmed. It was just a nightmare.

What had happened?

Slowly, she remembered. Morpheus had found them—her and Tazo, Hero, and Pecklion. They had been on the side of the mountain. Under the stars. Under the *horses*. But now, where was she? Where were the others?

She rubbed her eyes and peered around. It was dark, though not the same impenetrable darkness as the nightmare. The floor was damp, and the air smelled of mold. As her eyes adjusted, she could make out Hero lying beside her. They seemed to be in some sort of prison, for the wall in front of them was made of metal bars, and at the end sat a guard, hunched and thin. At the other end was a heavy wooden door, with a smaller door cut in it.

She couldn't see Tazo or Pecklion. She looked behind her, hoping she might glimpse them, only to gasp.

There were others in the darkness. Not horses. But others. *Enormous* others.

Pippa stood and took a step toward them, hardly daring to breathe.

Could it be?

There, in the shadows, their wrists and ankles wrapped in enormous chains fastened to the stone walls, were those whom all mortals both loved and feared. The gods and goddesses!

There was Athena, goddess of wisdom, her brown hair limp, her chiton muddied and torn, but her long graceful neck and high nose still raised proudly. Beside her, Aphrodite was chained too. Even in the squalor of the prison, she was beautiful in her simplicity, her chiton neither dyed nor decorated and her hair falling to the floor in golden tangles.

Near them was Hephaestus, god of blacksmiths, his scraggly beard snarled with bits of metal; and

Demeter, goddess of the harvest, bits of stray wheat caught in her hair. And there was Ares, god of war, who had caused Pippa so much strife during the race. For once he was without his silver helmet, the scars that crisscrossed his face gleaming white in the dim light. They were *all* there and clearly displeased.

"Hic . . . hic . . . hic . . ." Dionysus, god of festivities, was hiccupping uncontrollably. "What a *hic* punishment, trapped *hic* here without any wine. They could easily push a bottle through that little door."

"Punishment?" harped Ares. "Punishment is listening to you."

"Punishment is wearing the very chains you forged, locked within the very bars you constructed," said Hephaestus. "I never should have built this holding cell for Zeus. I told him Tartarus was enough of a dungeon."

"At least there it would be darker," complained another—who had to be Hades, based on his dark and gloomy demeanor and the serpent belt wrapped around his chiton. "I can't handle all this light."

"We'd better not be sent to Tartarus," spoke a goddess, who Pippa didn't recognize at first. She was very beautiful, with a crown of drooping peacock feathers.

"Or I'll never speak to my husband again!"

"Hera, dear," started Aphrodite.

Hera—Zeus's wife! "Don't dear me! The least Zeus could do is send some attendants. . . ."

"Attendants? Zeus? He has nothing now, like us," spat Ares.

"Then who *hic* are those over there?" Dionysus pointed right at Pippa.

"Those aren't attendants. I recognize that one," growled Ares, glancing at Pippa, his eyes catching hers and narrowing.

"Of course you do, Ares," said Aphrodite, her voice calm and soothing as ever. "It's Hippolyta from the race."

"Pah!" he spat. "But what is she doing here? And who is that with her?"

He gestured with his chin to the boy.

Hero stood up, shakily. "H-H—"

"Hero," said Pippa.

"Hero? That's your name? Ha! No mortal is ever really a hero," griped Ares.

Aphrodite ignored him. "My dear child," she said to Pippa. "What *are* you doing here?"

"I—we—came to return a winged horse."

"A winged horse? Here?" Athena's eyes brightened.

"He was taken from us, by Morpheus," said Pippa. "I was training him so Zeus could ride him, but we lost our map and then we were captured, and now Poseidon has him. I'm sure."

"Me?" came a bellowing voice from one corner of the prison. "I don't think so."

Pippa spun around. Her eyes went wide.

There, in a far corner all by himself, his ankles and wrists wrapped in triple the chains of the others, was the god of the sea.

Nineteen

"Poseidon?!" Pippa burst out.

Poseidon's beard, usually dripping with sea water and tangled with seaweed, was dry, but his eyes were surprisingly wet. His cloak, iridescent as an abalone shell, was torn and there was a gash across one of his cheeks.

Pippa didn't understand. "But you're the one who had us captured. You shouldn't be here. Zeus said . . ."

"Zeus doesn't know everything," interjected Athena.

"Zeus doesn't know *anything*," pouted Poseidon.

Athena glared at him. "Don't speak ill of Zeus. If *you* hadn't started all this . . ."

Poseidon slumped. "Yes, yes, I know. But this wasn't how it was supposed to turn out." He gazed at Pippa and Hero. "A mortal would understand. Have you not wanted to be someone other than yourself? Even for a day? Have you never felt that life treated you unfairly?"

Hero stiffened and stayed silent. Pippa was silent too. She had felt that way, of course. Many times.

"Yes, I see it in you both. Searching for who you truly are. It is a mortal's quest. So why not a god's too?"

"Because we are ideally suited to our roles!" said Athena.

"We *are* who we *are*!" roared Ares.

"You must learn to love yourself," added Aphrodite softly.

"I know that now," said Poseidon. "I would give anything to be back in the sea. But you can't place *all* the blame on me."

"What . . . what do you mean?" asked Hero.

"Nyx," replied the god.

"Nyx?" whispered Pippa. Goddess of the night?

The piece of darkness on the chariot—was that a piece of Nyx's cloak?

"I went to Nyx, in the Underworld, to get her help," explained Poseidon. "I knew the winged horses were the key to defeating Zeus. Without a horse—his or any other—he would struggle to find a way to attack with his lightning bolts. So I sought Nyx, the goddess with the power to transform the horses. I wanted her help to get rid of them, at least for now, so I could take the throne." He rubbed his beard. "Why should Zeus be king and not me, his brother, or one of our other siblings? Nyx understood. Her daughter, Hermera, goddess of day, brags relentlessly about how much brighter she is than her mother. Which meant that Nyx was only too happy to add more stars, more constellations, to brighten her sky.

"All was well, at first. With the winged horses gone, I *easily* seized the throne—"

"Ahem," coughed Ares.

"Well, yes, there was the darkness. Nyx did help with that. And getting the relics," said Poseidon. "But I filled the palace with sea monsters, as well as the winged horse stables, didn't I? And I couldn't know she and her children were going to put you all in the dungeon.

I was deciding how best to help my brothers and sisters when—"

"Ha!" interjected Athena. *"Help."*

Poseidon ignored her. "—when Nyx appeared again. The extra stars had blinded her to anything but her own glory. She turned on me too. She cast another spell of darkness and took my relic. She has them all now."

"My spear and helmet!" griped Ares.

"My *hiccup* cup," added Dionysus.

"Your cup is *not* a relic," admonished Athena. "Not like my owl."

"Or my trident," continued Poseidon. "Then Nyx imprisoned us here."

"Isn't there anything you can do?" cried Pippa.

"Not without our relics, and not in these chains," said Poseidon.

"You're not in chains," said Aphrodite, staring at Pippa's wrists. "Perhaps you can do something."

A grim voice came from nearby: "Mortals save *you*? That almost makes me laugh."

The prison guard had turned her chair toward them. She had a face that looked like it had never worn a smile, and she was thin as a skeleton, with stringy hair and sharpened teeth. She reminded Pippa of a splinter or thorn, the kind a horse might have in his hoof, causing slow and perpetual pain. She leaned on a cane of metal. No, not a cane. It was a key.

"You will be stuck here forever or until my mother moves you to Tartarus, the prison of the Underworld. And I will be stuck too, watching over you until the world ends. I will languish and no one will care, not even my mother." The guard's lips trembled, and her eyes filled with tears—black tears—that spilled down her face.

Pippa shrunk back, nearly stumbling into Aphrodite.

"That is Achlys, goddess of misery, one of the daughters of Nyx," said Aphrodite. "She has the particular effect of spreading woe, especially to mortals. It's best if you ignore her."

But it was too late. Looking upon Achlys and hearing her words had planted a seed of despair in Pippa. She suddenly found herself worrying about Tazo, thinking the worst. He wasn't there, so that meant Nyx had him and it was only a matter of time before he, too, was turned to stars . . . if he hadn't been already.

"So there's no way to escape?" said Pippa, struggling against the urge to cry.

"Perhaps one day," said Aphrodite hopefully. "If we believe and keep love in our hearts."

"*Love!* Ha! Love will never free us," roared Ares. "Especially not if we are moved to Tartarus."

As the gods and goddesses began to bicker, Pippa huddled with Hero.

"One day to the gods and goddesses could be *centuries* to us," said Pippa. "We'll never escape."

Hero, however, pointed to the little door, built within the big one, that seemed to be for providing prisoners with food and drink. "It's large enough for us to crawl through."

"We can't slip through there, not with Achlys on guard," said Pippa. "And it probably doesn't matter anyway. Tazo is likely turned to stars, or dead," she choked. "It's . . . it's all my fault. I should have stayed in the mortal realm. A trip to the temple would be a better fate for Tazo than what's in store for him now."

"Hey, hey," hushed Hero.

But it was too late. A tear slipped out from her eye.

"Ah," breathed Achlys. "You are crying. Crying

because you are in the dungeon. Come, let me wipe your eyes." She extended a long fingernail, cracked and dirty.

Pippa clutched Hero's hand and shrank back farther.

"Of course, you are frightened of me. I am frightening. I am disgusting," said Achlys. "That's right, you should stay back, far away from me." And with that, Achlys, goddess of misery, slumped against the key, her head hanging toward the floor.

Pippa let out a sigh of relief. But Hero didn't. Instead, he stood up tall, a glimmer in his eyes.

"Pippa," he whispered, "I have an idea."

Twenty

"Misery loves company," Hero whispered.

"What do you mean?" Pippa asked.

Hero opened his mouth as though to explain, then shook his head. "You'll see." With that, he strode toward the bars, toward Achlys.

"It's time to tell my story—the real one," he began as he sat down on the floor in front of the guard. She didn't say anything, didn't even look up.

"My story begins before I was born," Hero said. "My great-great-great-grandfather was Hercules, the legendary hero. My family worshipped him as if he were Zeus.

When my mother was pregnant with me, an oracle told my father that I would be the next hero in our family."

Achlys still didn't look up. "Go away," she said.

Hero ignored her and continued, "My father, determined that I should follow in Hercules's footsteps, placed two deadly snakes in my cradle, hoping I would strangle them with my bare hands, like Hercules did when he was a baby."

Behind Pippa, the gods and goddesses had quieted their fighting, and she could tell they were listening to Hero's story now, puzzled as to what he was doing.

"Of course, I couldn't strangle them," said Hero. "I wasn't like Hercules. I was just an ordinary baby! One of them bit me."

"N-no!" stammered Achlys, who finally looked up at him.

"I should have died then. I almost did. But I lived—barely. I was sick and weak all through my childhood. I didn't have any friends. No one wanted to play with me." A tear trickled from one of Hero's eyes.

Achlys reached a hand through the bars and caught the tear on her fingertip.

Hero didn't flinch at her touch. "Things only

grew worse. My father continued to test me, to give me impossible challenges. I stood no chance. I was—I *am*—my father's biggest disappointment."

Tears were now streaming from both his eyes, and Pippa felt her eyes getting wet as well. How could a parent do these things?

"When my brother was born," continued Hero, "he was everything my father wanted. He looked like a hero. And he was stronger than me."

Achlys now hung on his every word. Tears streamed from her eyes too. "That is a sad story." She reached through the bars and clasped Hero's hands in her own. The key fell to the floor with a clang. Hero let her touch him and even squeezed her hands back. "Tell me more," said Achlys.

All at once, Pippa understood. *Misery loves company.* Hero was keeping Achlys company, keeping her occupied, to give Pippa a chance.

Hero kept talking. "Soon, both my brother and my father were ordering me about, making me do all the tasks in our oikos they did not want to do. I was forced to do their bidding, until I decided to do something about it. . . ."

Pippa wanted to stay and hear more, but she couldn't waste this opportunity. She crept, as quietly as she could, to the far end of the bars where the small door was and knelt down, half listening to Hero as he went on.

"I stole my father's most prized possession, the Nemean cloak, *Hercules's* cloak. And I traveled here to prove him and my brother wrong."

"So your story changes into a happy one?" complained Achlys.

Pippa froze, fearing that Achlys, no longer distracted by the sad tale, might return her attention to the prisoners and spy her.

Hero seemed to sense this and let out a loud sob. It sounded fake, but as he continued, his crying began to sound genuine.

"Does it look like I am wearing the cloak?" choked Hero. "No. Everything has gone wrong."

"It has?" said Achlys. Once again, tears filled her eyes. "Tell me, tell me."

No wonder Hero was so upset when the cloak was lost; it wasn't really his, Pippa thought, and wished she could tell him she was sorry, that he *was* a hero to put up with that kind of father, to be so positive despite all he'd been through. It even made sense now, why Tazo and Pecklion seemed to like Hero so much. Not because he was like Hercules but because he wasn't. He wasn't some creature-slaying hero. He was just a boy, like Bas. But now was not the time to tell Hero all of this.

Pippa pushed open the door flap, which was big enough for a plate of god-size food—or a small mortal. Slowly, slowly, on hands and knees, Pippa crept through.

She was free! She stood up, her heart pounding, and gave a furtive glance back at the cell and the gods and goddesses.

Aphrodite was smiling. Athena nodded. "Go!" she mouthed.

While Hero continued his story and Achlys cried, Pippa ran, as lightly as if she were a winged horse skimming the ground, holding her breath until she rounded the corner and the prison disappeared from sight.

The hallway was dark, lit by only a few oil lamps built into the walls. A set of massive stairs loomed in front of her.

As she struggled up them, her thoughts spun. She was free, but now what? She couldn't stop Nyx by herself. She *could* tell Zeus all she'd learned. And maybe she could rescue Tazo—if Nyx hadn't already turned him into stars.

At the top of the stairs, she gasped. A grand marble hallway stretched as far as she could see. The ceiling reached so high it felt like she was staring up at a milky-colored sky. Mosaics made of gemstones decorated the walls in swirling images of the gods and goddesses performing great feats. Athena offering the olive tree to a mortal. Poseidon creating the first horse with his powerful trident. Aphrodite rising from the sea in a giant scallop shell. Hera's apple tree—the fruit so red she was tempted to reach out and pick it.

Pippa had never been inside the gods' palace. Most of her previous time on the mountain had been spent training Zeph. Once, she and the riders had been invited to the palace for a feast, but the gods and goddesses had been fighting and so it was canceled. *Did the gods ever stop fighting?* wondered Pippa. She hadn't been to the great ceremony at the end of the race either because she and Bas had been disqualified and sent home.

Where would Nyx keep Tazo? Perhaps on the roof?

She had to hurry. Who knew how long Hero's story would keep Achlys occupied.

Pippa ran down the hall, searching for stairs, slipping off her sandals because they made too much noise—especially when she encountered puddles of water, hints that sea monsters had been living here. Seaweed hung from some of the mosaics, and salt crusted on the walls in white swirling patterns.

But there were no actual monsters. No sirens or hippocampi or hydra. Whenever she came to a corner, she listened for voices. If Nyx had employed her daughter, Achlys, to guard the prisoners, and her son, Morpheus, to patrol the mountain, she probably had other children roaming the palace, doing her bidding. Nyx *had* birthed many of the gods and goddesses. Pippa couldn't remember them all, but she knew Nyx had been around even before Zeus.

None of Nyx's children were wandering the halls, however. No one was. The corridors seemed to go on forever, each more magnificent than the last and just as empty. Pippa imagined all the gods and goddesses and their attendants filling up the space and how different it must be.

She slowed when she reached a hall decorated with winged horses soaring between blue-tiled clouds and the ceiling: a mosaic of the race. She couldn't help following the horses until the hall ended in a court-yard.

There, a fountain bubbled, not with water but with a shimmering liquid that smelled so sweet it made her mouth water.

Ambrosia! The drink of the gods and goddesses. The drink of immortality.

Ambrosia made a mortal into a demigod or demi-goddess. If she took just one sip, she would be like Sophia. She could live on the mountain forever.

One sip, and she wouldn't have to worry about the future anymore. She wouldn't have to return to les-sons and impractical clothing and acting like a proper young lady.

The smell was intoxicating. Pippa took a step for-ward, and another. Before she realized it, she was standing over the fountain, the liquid right below her, bubbling like music.

She dipped her hands into it and cupped a mouth-ful, watching it change colors in her hands—first red like wine, then blue like the sea, then gold like the sun.

If she was immortal, she'd be able to find out her own answers. Being immortal would solve everything.

Or would it?

If she was immortal she'd have to stay on the mountain—with the gods. Zeph lived below. Would she ever see him again?

A distant whinny broke the hold the sweet-smelling substance had over her.

Tazo!

Pippa separated her hands, the ambrosia spilling back into the fountain.

The whinny came again. Ambrosia was not the answer. Not now.

She ran from the courtyard, toward the sound, past columns of gold and silver, past statues that looked only a step away from being alive, past trees growing like a forest from the stones, to a room that wasn't really a room because it didn't have a roof but opened straight into the sky.

There, in robes of sky herself, with wings of woven stars, was the great goddess Nyx.

Twenty-one

Pippa froze in the doorway.

Nyx was standing in the middle of the room, her back to Pippa. The tips of her folded wings brushed the earth. In front of the goddess, Pippa could just make out Tazo. He hadn't been turned to stars yet! Pecklion was tied in a corner, his ears pressed back and his rooster's comb sticking straight up in fear.

"Fly! Fly!" Nyx shouted at Tazo.

Tazo's wings lifted, but he didn't move.

"Stupid horse!" Nyx spat. "You're the last of your kind and yet you will not fly! FLY!" she demanded.

Tazo's body trembled and his wings quivered.

"Pah! I have had enough of you." Nyx pulled out a whip from her robes. It looked like a giant black snake. "You shall be the dimmest star in my sky," she declared.

The goddess of night raised the whip over her head.

Pippa leaped from the doorway. "NO!" she cried. Nyx turned and glared.

Now that Pippa was face-to-face with her, she could see the goddess in all her glory.

Her hair was black, streaked with glittering white as if shooting stars had fallen through it, and a glowing moon hung around her neck. Her lips were lush and deep crimson, the color of summer sunsets. Although Nyx was goddess of night, of darkness, Pippa couldn't imagine a more radiant being. Even her eyes were white, with no trace of black.

She pointed her whip at Pippa.

"Mortal!" she said, her voice full of venom. "You escaped."

Pippa stuck her hand in her pocket, clutching her coin for courage.

"Perhaps I should dispose of mortals altogether. All they do is cause trouble." Nyx raised her whip again.

"Don't hurt him!" Pippa cried.

"Him? *Ha!* First you, then him!" Nyx laughed, and brought the whip snapping down.

It cracked across Pippa's body, and for a moment, there was a blinding flash. She heard a distant whinny and felt a shock buzz through her body.

She was sure this was it. Everything was over. But when the flash faded, she was still there, Nyx hovering over her, whip in hand.

"Impossible!" cried Nyx. "How did you not transform?"

Slowly Pippa sat up. She wasn't dead or turned into stars. In fact, she wasn't hurt at all. Only a small spot of her dress had been burned away, the pocket with her coin in it. She felt for it, and the coin fell out with a clink, rolling across the marble floor.

"What's this?" Nyx stepped on the coin to stop it from rolling. She picked it up and flipped it between her long fingers. "I know this."

She threw the coin back at Pippa, who scrambled to catch it.

"So you are the child of the winged horse thieves."

"Winged horse thieves?" Pippa faltered, clutching her coin tightly. Images flashed in her mind—the statue that marked the Graveyard of Wings, the coin around Euippe's neck that was identical to hers. Euippe had recognized Pippa although she'd never seen her before. Was that what Euippe was trying to tell her? Could it be? Were Pippa's parents the mortals who had helped heal the injured winged horses? At last, after all this time, had she really found out who her parents were, from Nyx herself?

"You must be," continued Nyx, "if you carry that coin. It was the token they left in the night to let each other know a new horse was ready. And I suppose it is a powerful protective charm too. But you can't protect yourself forever. At least your parents couldn't."

Nyx's beautiful lips curled back in a grimace. "Everyone uses my darkness to commit their bad deeds, and I was—I *am*—sick and tired of it! I put an end to your parents' thievery. Yes, I remember that night. I made it so dark that those mortals were lost—not for hours, or days, but for forever. First the man, then the woman. I thought the child had died too. I didn't know you lived."

Pippa remembered her terrible nightmare, the feeling of darkness so heavy it was suffocating. And the kiss—it must have been her mother's last.

She could see it all now. Euippe ready to meet her father with an injured winged horse. Her father heading out from the stables into the darkness. When he didn't come back, her mother must have gone after him. She must have left Pippa by the well, with the protective coin. But the darkness—Nyx's darkness—had swallowed her mother too.

Pippa couldn't believe it. She wasn't ever meant to be a regular girl. She had always been meant to work with winged horses, just like her parents.

All at once, Pippa knew who she was.

She wasn't a foundling or a racer, or a proper young lady. She was Hippolyta, lover of horses.

She felt strong and certain inside. And angry.

"You killed my parents!" she cried. "*You* are using the darkness for evil."

"They deserved their fate," spat Nyx. Her dark eyes narrowed. "They were meddling. Meddling with the gods' horses."

"No!" cried Pippa. "Euippe told me the story. They were caring for the hurt ones. When the horses were better, they sent them *back* to Mount Olympus. They were *helping* the horses. And the night was helping them!"

"No," said Nyx, gripping her whip as if to use it again, but her voice quavered.

Nyx's uncertainty gave Pippa an idea. The goddess had revealed to Pippa who Pippa truly was, even though it was only by accident. Maybe Pippa could do the same, but on purpose. Maybe she could remind Nyx of what night could be.

"Yes, the night was *helping* them!" said Pippa. "Night is beautiful. It's not just for bad deeds or nightmares. It's for dreams too. Night is for relaxing. For resting. Night is the best part of the day, saved till last. . . ."

Nyx was softening, her grip on the whip loosening. Pippa kept going.

"Night isn't a place for bad deeds, unless you make it so. The stars will be a constant reminder of *your* bad deed. I know you don't want that. Please, let the winged horses go," urged Pippa.

For a moment, Pippa thought Nyx might really do it.

"*Please*," said Pippa. "You can't see yourself truly, because you aren't yourself. You're too bright. . . ."

"Too bright?!" Nyx's face twisted up. Pippa had gone too far. "TOO BRIGHT?!" Nyx repeated.

She cast out her whip again, and it was like she didn't even care where she was hitting.

Pecklion screeched, Tazo reared.

"Stop! Stop!" Pippa cried.

"Stop? I am only doing this pathetic horse a favor! He does not belong here on Olympus, nor does he belong down in the mortal realm. The sky should take him," roared Nyx.

"He isn't a pathetic horse!" said Pippa. "He's the colt of the true winner of the last Winged Horse Race. I bet—I bet . . . I bet he is faster than any of the others!"

Tazo perked his ears and looked at her.

"You bet?" Nyx stilled her whip. Her eyes glinted even brighter.

Pippa's mind spun furiously. Her first plan hadn't worked. But Nyx wasn't just Night, she was also a goddess. And Sophia had said, "No god or goddess can refuse a bet."

"Yes, I bet! I bet he is the fastest!" Pippa continued bravely.

"Really?! You think *this* horse is the fastest? Ha! You want the winged horses?"

"Yes!" said Pippa.

Maybe Nyx would bring the horses down to prove her wrong.

But Nyx had another idea.

"Then we shall race." Nyx tucked her whip into the

belt around her peplos. "If you touch the stars first, the horses are yours. If you don't, your horse and *you* will become my next constellation."

Pippa gulped.

Tazo had never flown with her on his back, much less raced. How could they win? Still, she had to have hope.

After all, he *was* Zeph's colt. And he was Tazo. A promise.

Twenty-two

Nyx opened her wings and a burst of wind from them pushed Pippa backward. Pippa couldn't help staring. They were the most beautiful wings she'd seen, black and silver softly melding into each other, like comet tails streaking through the midnight sky.

Pippa hoisted herself onto Tazo's back. She took a few deep breaths, trying to stay calm.

Flying in the Winged Horse Race was one thing. If you lost, or even cheated, you returned to the mortal realm, back to your old life, no worse off than when you began. This was different. It was a game to Nyx. She was a goddess. But for Pippa, two lives were at stake: hers and Tazo's.

"Whatever happens, I love you," she leaned down and whispered in Tazo's ear.

"When I crack my whip, that will be the signal for the race to begin," said the goddess. "Do you think you need a head start?" she cackled.

"No," said Pippa, more certain than she felt.

"Good," said Nyx. "Because you are not getting one!"

SNAP!

A blaze of light blinded Pippa, who feared for a moment that Nyx had gone back on her word and transformed Tazo right then and there, or maybe Pecklion.

When the light dimmed, Nyx was revealed, erupting up and out through the open ceiling.

"Fly! Fly, Tazo!" cried Pippa, urging him on with her body.

But Tazo didn't move. Desperately, she tried to think of a solution. The only time he'd flown was when he'd chased after the escaped nightmare, curious about the shimmering flying object, just like Zeph would have been. But there was nothing to chase now, nothing that didn't frighten him. Unless . . . her coin! She tossed it up, as high as she could.

The coin glinted.

Whether it was the coin, or her urging, or her knees pressing into his side, Pippa didn't know. Tazo opened his wings, took a few bounding strides, and *WHOOSH!* He was off! He soared out of the palace, and into the sky.

As the coin arced in the air, Nyx looked over her shoulder, surprise on her face. "You can fly!"

Indeed, Tazo could!

His wings beat powerfully, his neck straining forward. Although the coin was falling back down to the throne room floor, Tazo didn't seem to care. He ascended magnificently, as though eager to show himself off, to prove just how strong his wings were, as though he was saying, "I *am* a winged horse! Yes, I can fly—and look how well!"

Pippa was filled with pride and, at the same time, terror.

Nyx was ahead of them, not as far ahead as she might be, but still ahead.

"*Faster,*" Pippa urged Tazo.

Nyx's wings sparkled. As big and strong as they

seemed, Nyx wasn't as fast as Pippa had thought. *Perhaps we do have a chance.*

She leaned close to Tazo, her cheek pressed against his neck, as they went up, up, up. Already they were far higher than she'd ever flown on Zeph.

The goddess was just a bit in front of them now. Ahead was a wispy ribbon of cloud. As they approached it, they were nose to nose with the beautiful goddess. And then, a nose ahead. They were doing it, really doing it; they were passing Nyx. . . .

But then they flew through the thin clouds, and suddenly, everything was different. It was as if the clouds had been a gate into the sky realm. All at once, the air was thin, and it was hard to breathe. The stars glimmered a hundred times bigger and brighter than before, like lakes of light in a black expanse.

Nyx spun around, flying backward so she could face them, and kicked her feet at them. "You really think you can beat me? Me, goddess of night? Brighter than day?"

She laughed and the laugh seemed to echo off the stars.

"I do admit you have speed. Perhaps below you would have had a chance. Not up here. Not in *my* world.

You were right. That horse is a fine steed. You and he will make a very valuable constellation indeed." She laughed again, hovering and dancing around Pippa.

Pippa struggled to breathe. Tazo too was struggling, his wingbeats slowing.

The stars looked so big. Yet they were still too far away to touch. She would never be able to reach them. She could see the horses clearly now. The stars of their wings quivered as they pranced back and forth across the darkness. Pippa could make out the large and graceful Ajax, and the golden, radiant Khruse.

"Give up! Admit it, you've lost," crowed Nyx, turning around and continuing toward the constellations.

Fury filled Pippa. This wasn't a bet. This was a trick! Nyx had known that all along. Pippa felt despair—the same despair she had in the cell. She had let everyone down, especially Tazo. He might not be Zeph, but she loved him with all her heart. She had promised to keep him safe.

Pippa remembered the first time she'd touched his soft nose. How she had to lure him with figs. He had come to her, not only because of the figs, but because he trusted her. She couldn't have gone to him. That would have only frightened the little colt.

Suddenly, a thought, bright as a star itself, filled her.

She didn't have to go to the horses. They could come to her!

And she had just the way.

The whistle. Bellerophon's whistle, that hung around her neck, that had hung there since she'd picked it up in the pool of water a day ago. It might not call Tazo, but it would call the other horses.

She let go of a handful of Tazo's mane and reached for the whistle. Although she could barely breathe in the thin air, she managed to draw in a wheezing breath and, summoning every bit of strength she could, she pursed her lips and blew.

TWEET!

The high birdlike call filled the air, and for a moment everything seemed to freeze.

The stars shone brighter, brighter, brighter, and began to fall, streaming down toward them. A hundred shooting stars all falling together.

The horses!

Tazo whinnied in fear. Nyx screeched as they streaked past her in a *V*, avoiding her completely, heading straight for Pippa and Tazo. The goddess was stunned into stillness.

Pippa put out her hand, but closed her eyes, sure she was going to be blinded or killed by the stars, and then . . .

She felt the brush of feathers.

She opened her eyes. Zeus's majestic steed, Ajax, now a horse, not stars, brushed by her. He whinnied and tossed his head, but he didn't stop. He raced down, down, his wings beating like music.

And he was just the first.

All it had taken was one touch. The stars were horses now, a herd of winged horses, flying past her. Khruse, as golden as the sun. Hali, with his mane and tail that shimmered ocean blue. Skotos, so slim and black he could be mistaken for a shadow. The fire steeds of Helios, with their flame-feathered wings. And the saffron-rose horses of Eos, goddess of dawn. Even Aurae, whom as a foal, Pippa had seen take her first flight, now bigger than Tazo himself.

The winged horses were back.

A hundred beautiful horses, swooping down like a rainbow toward Mount Olympus.

Twenty-three

As the last of the horses passed by Pippa and Tazo, something more sinister came streaking from above. Even without the added starlight, Pippa could see Nyx, plunging through the air toward them.

Pippa turned Tazo, and they began to soar down, but the goddess was quicker. She pulled out of her dive and stopped in front of Pippa and Tazo, blocking their way.

"How dare you!" she cried. "You tricked me!"

"That wasn't a trick!" Pippa replied. "You said who-ever *touches* them first. Not who reaches them."

"Words, words, words!" Nyx drew out her whip. "At least I will have one new constellation to decorate my sky."

"That isn't fair! I touched the stars first! That was our bet!" retorted Pippa, as Tazo struggled to beat against the force of Nyx's wings.

"What of life is fair?" spat Nyx.

"Some things!" said Pippa.

"Nothing!" cried Nyx. "It would be *fair* if my sky were as bright as my daughter's. If Poseidon ruled with his brother."

"Some things can't be," continued Pippa. "If everything was fair, then everything would be the same. And who would decide what was fair, anyway?"

"*Me!*" raged Nyx. She raised her whip high.

CRACK!

A blinding flash split the darkness.

"No!" Nyx screeched, as a lightning bolt blazed across the sky.

Tazo startled, and Pippa gripped at his mane as he struggled to regain his balance. When at last he had, she looked down and saw in the distance—just a speck at first but growing bigger with every passing moment—Zeus!

Zeus on the back of Ajax. Joy surged through Pippa.

In one hand the god of the mountain held another lightning bolt, ready to throw. His great beard crackled with sparks.

"HUZZAH!" he cried.

Nyx cast her whip.

SNAP! CRACK!

The air shuddered, and Pippa was blinded by a white light. Tazo tried to rear, but with nothing under his hooves, he looped completely upside down. Pippa's stomach looped too, as she frantically clung to his mane. In a heartbeat, he was right-side up again, but her joy had fled with the realization that she was caught in the middle of a battle!

Zeus wasn't alone.

Poseidon was galloping upward toward his brother on sea-blue Hali, wielding his trident. Close behind followed Athena, a sword in each hand. She was riding a mare that looked more owl than horse, with a beak for a muzzle and wings of gray. Ares sat on a steed that looked like fearsome Kerauno's colt, for it had bloodred eyes and pointed teeth. The war god's silver helmet was back on his head, and his spear in hand. Even Aphrodite flew with them, astride a steed the color of sunbeams.

"Hooray for Hero!" Poseidon cried. "Achlys didn't stand a chance."

So Hero had found a way to free them too!

This was no time to ask how, or if Hero was okay. Not that they would hear her. The gods and goddesses didn't seem to notice her at all—especially as Nyx's children joined the battle. First came Morpheus, who was flying by the strength of his wings, much as it might tire him. Pippa didn't recognize all the others, but they were surely the sons and daughters of the goddess of night, for they flocked around her.

A tiny shriveled god, who clung to an equally shriveled winged horse. A goddess with a crooked smile, who was invisible one moment and visible the next. Another goddess who wielded a whip like her mother's in one hand and an apple branch in the other, and whose face was half green. Last of all, a god with wings like Nyx's yet completely black swooped past her. He carried a torch, but the torch was upside down and extinguished. Pippa shuddered. She knew the symbol of Thanatos, god of death.

She tried to turn Tazo away from the terrible Thanatos, but Demeter, goddess of the harvest, cut them off. She threw a stalk of wheat that burst open upon the god, covering him with tiny growing shoots. He cried out, knocking them away as best he could with his torch.

When Pippa turned Tazo the other way, she was blocked by another battling pair: a fanged and taloned goddess, whose face was ravaged by disease, and Aphrodite, on the back of the sunbeam horse. Pippa didn't know what the goddess of love would fight with. To her surprise, Aphrodite pulled out a bow and arrow, the same sort Pippa imagined her son Cupid used, and shot at the fanged goddess, who flew away screeching.

No matter which way Tazo went, there was no clear path of escape. Pippa tried to stay on as the colt looped and rolled and struggled to dodge the spells and weapons that flew back and forth.

"Pippa!" cried a familiar voice.

Pippa turned to see Sophia swooping beside her, on the back of what had to be one of Helios's winged steeds. Eurippe was on her other side, riding a fire horse as well. The two steeds had wings that flickered and spit like fires, with white-gold feathers. Sophia and Eurippe didn't seem to notice the heat shimmering from their horses, though even Pippa could feel it.

"The steeds came to us!" cried Sophia, grinning. "You're a marvel!"

"Oh, Sophia!" Pippa exclaimed.

But her friend and Eurippe were off, two blazing fires fighting in the darkness, and Pippa, distracted by their leaving, didn't see Morpheus upon her until it was too late.

Then there was another bright blaze, this one cold and white, and a *CRACK*—the third one directed at her—followed by a flash. And this time she could not avoid them. There was no white light, no nightmare either, just darkness. Total darkness . . .

Twenty-four

Pippa was woken by sunbeams streaming through a window in front of her. The sun! The sun was back, not shining dimly at the edge of the horizon but high in the sky where it belonged.

Slowly, she sat up. She was in a bed of hay. Her dirty dress was gone, and instead she wore a chiton made of the lightest, finest threads she could imagine. It was delicately embroidered with a pattern of tiny silver wings. Pippa touched it in wonder.

Where was she? The last thing she remembered was being trapped between opposing sides in the battle.

Cautiously, she looked around. The room was small, unadorned except for a single weaving—a very strange one—hanging on the wall. It looked more like a mess of knots than anything else. If she squinted though, she could see it was some sort of rose. Or maybe a shell. Or the sun? Every time it seemed to change.

Through the open doorway came low voices and the smell of food. She got up, carefully, and made her way toward them. Her head felt fuzzy and she had to hold on to the side of the doorway to steady herself.

The room, like several others, opened up into a little courtyard, built in the shape of a horseshoe, with a cistern in the center. Grapevines grew on a trellis overhead, providing shade. Except in one corner, where a fire crackled. An old woman was hunched over the fire, poking the contents of a pot with a spoon.

In another corner was a table surrounded by stools and a spindle. A second old woman sat at the spindle, and a third at the table, along with a boy, who was eating soup.

Hero and the Fates!

"Oh, dearie, you're up!" said Clotho, not looking up from the spindle yet somehow knowing Pippa was there.

"Pippa!" exclaimed Hero.

Pippa smiled and made her way to them, unsteadily.

"Sit, sit," said Clotho. "Before you fall over."

"Humph. She's lucky she can stand at all. No thanks to the gods." Atropos waved her hands wildly, and Hero ducked just in time, narrowly avoiding being stabbed with her shears. "No one ever thinks practically. No one ever thinks of the mortals!"

"What happened?" asked Pippa, sitting down.

"You were hit by dream dust. You're lucky Hero caught you," said Clotho.

"He did?" Pippa gazed, surprised, at Hero.

"It—it was Pecklion, actually," he stammered.

"But how did you get out of the prison?" asked Pippa. "How did all the gods and goddesses get out?"

"Hero again," smiled Clotho.

Hero's blush deepened. "It really wasn't me." He turned to Pippa. "Misery was so happy to have company at last and felt so sorry for me, she decided to let me go, to let us all go. She didn't want to work for her mother anymore. Then, well, the gods and goddesses burst out and found their relics. Just as they were wondering what to do with them, the horses came. That was your doing. *You* rescued the horses.

"Sophia wants to write up both of us in her scroll," Hero went on. "She says there's a new section, the horse rescuers. She wanted to tell you that. I told her it should just be about you. I mean, I've always admired you . . . I was even jealous of you a little. . . ."

Pippa wasn't sure what surprised her more. That Hero was jealous of her or that she'd be in Sophia's scroll.

"You saved everyone," finished Hero.

"We both did, Hero," said Pippa firmly.

Hero smiled slowly.

"And Tazo's okay?" Pippa asked.

"He's in the garden," said Clotho, "with the hippalektryon. They have been eating since they got here. It's so nice to have our garden back. As soon as we could, we moved houses. I must say that stone house does chill the fingers. It isn't easy to spin with cold fingers, you know."

Pippa was about to ask how long she'd been there, when, from her place at the pot, Lachesis waved her wooden spoon. "Do you think the soup needs more olives?"

"More olives? Oh, goodness me, no," replied Clotho. "Maybe more grapes. What do you think, Hero?"

Hero looked up from his bowl, and Pippa could tell he was trying desperately not to grimace. "I suppose."

"And, when you're done, serve Pippa a bowl too, sister," said Clotho.

"I'm actually not hungry," blurted Pippa.

"Tut, tut," said Clotho. "I can hear your stomach growling from here. The soup will do you good."

"*Soup?*" a loud voice bellowed from outside.

"Oh dear, it's—" started Clotho.

"You-know-who," finished Lachesis.

"Really, if all these gods and goddesses keep visiting, we will need a bigger house," huffed Atropos, just as Zeus ducked through the entryway.

He strode into the courtyard. Although there were no lightning bolts in his hands, he still crackled with energy. His frizzy beard spread out around him like a cloud. Gone were his crutch and bandage. His robes were no longer creased but flowed around him as though blown by a wind that only he could feel. The god of the sky, king of the gods was back, and Pippa couldn't help feeling in awe of his majestic presence.

When she saw his eyes twinkle, she relaxed.

"Soup! I'd love a bowl!" He took the one Lachesis had just ladled out, much to Pippa's relief, and gulped the soup down in one swallow. He coughed, and his beard seemed to deflate slightly.

"Good?" questioned Lachesis.

"Well . . . ," said Zeus.

"Here, have some more." The Fate reached for his empty bowl.

"Ah," he faltered, "as much as I'd like to, I'm here for Hippolyta and Hero." He glanced at them. "Join me for a walk?"

Pippa and Hero nodded quickly.

"Good," crackled Atropos. "It's too cramped in here. And enough with the soup, Lachesis. You're falling behind!" She pointed to a jumble of thread waiting to be measured.

While Lachesis reluctantly set down her soup and picked up her measuring stick, Zeus, Pippa, and Hero headed outside.

Outside, the sun felt warm and wonderful on Pippa's cheeks.

Ajax was grazing with Tazo and Pecklion in the garden. When Pippa passed, Tazo raised his head and wings, as though remembering their flight. Pippa waved at him, then hurried to catch up with Hero and Zeus, who were striding down the path into the rolling meadows.

The grass was lush and green, and dotted with wildflowers. *It's like the salt storm never happened,* thought Pippa. *Is this Zeus's doing? Or did all the gods and goddesses work together?*

Pippa closed her eyes and took a deep breath. She hadn't realized just how much she'd missed the sun.

Zeus coughed again. "Those Fates mean well, but . . ." He took a deep breath too. "Ah! Olympus. My Olympus!"

He paused, then corrected himself, *"Our* Olympus. I shall be including my brother Poseidon in more of my decision-making."

"Poseidon isn't going to be punished?" asked Hero, looking surprised.

"Ha!" burst Zeus. "Of course he is. Bellerophon has devised a most appropriate task for him and Nyx."

"Bellerophon's back?" burst Pippa.

"Never left," said Zeus. "He was always in the winged horse stables. The water monsters had him imprisoned there."

"And the stables?"

Zeus smiled. "They shall be gleaming in time. Until then, the horses have been moved elsewhere."

Pippa knew there were other stables dotted across the vast mountain and wondered if Zeus meant the foals' stables, where she'd seen Aurae take her first flight. If the winged horse steeds were housed there, maybe the foals and colts would be gentled, as Euippe had taught her it was important to do.

Euippe. Sophia. Pippa was about to ask about them, when Zeus stopped under a beautiful olive tree—a rarity on the mountain—and said, "Enough of punishments. That isn't why I am here. I am here to . . . to . . ."

He struggled to find the words. "You know what I am trying to say."

Pippa didn't. She looked at Hero. He looked confused too.

"Just say it!" came a faraway voice, back from the Fates' house.

Zeus cleared his throat and gazed deep into Pippa's

and Hero's eyes. "Thank you. Thank you both."

Pippa felt a tingle rush through her body. She couldn't believe it. The king of the gods, thanking *them*?

Then Zeus pulled something from his robes, two glass bottles that shimmered with all the colors of the rainbow. "This is a gift, so you can become a demigod and -goddess," started Zeus.

Zeus didn't have to finish for Pippa to guess. . . .

"Ambrosia?" breathed Pippa.

But she shook her head. Hero did too.

Zeus's bushy eyebrows shot up in disbelief. "Surely you jest? What better reward than becoming a demigod and demigoddess?"

"Hercules was a demigod," said Hero quietly. "But I don't want to be like Hercules anymore."

"You won't be Hercules. You will be Hero, the great . . . hero," said Zeus.

Pippa had to stifle a laugh.

"Exactly," said Hero. "It doesn't sound right, does it?"

Zeus turned to Pippa. "You, Hippolyta, surely you want to stay here, with us?"

"I thought that was what I wanted once. But now I have Zeph and I am part of Bas's family. And, there's something else."

"Ah, there *is* something you desire. Tell me. I will make it so."

Pippa gulped. You didn't ask for a gift from the gods. You gave them presents, yes. But ask for one? Still, why not. She had rescued the horses, after all. She was Hippolyta, lover of horses. She stood up a little straighter.

Pippa pointed back in the direction of the Fates' house. "I would like Tazo to return with me."

Zeus nodded.

"And I want him to keep his wings."

"Wings in the mortal realm?" said Zeus. He clucked his tongue, thinking. "Can you manage?"

"My parents could, and so can I, if I'm given the choice."

"Your parents. Of course . . . That reminds me." He reached into his robes again. This time he produced a coin. Her winged horse coin. It looked brighter than ever, as if some of the falling stars had covered it with stardust.

"I found this in my throne room, and I knew it must belong to you. Your parents were the mortals who tended my winged horses? Your parents . . . I never met them. I didn't know they had a child . . . Yes, you will care for Tazo well. I can see that."

That reminded Pippa of something else she wanted.

As she took the coin from him, she said, "I want you to promise me, no more senseless killing of winged horses."

Zeus nodded again.

"And let Euippe return to the surface to be a groom with Bellerophon again."

"That has already been done, but . . ."

"And I want you to apologize to her for what you did." She was on a roll now.

"Apologize?"

"Yes," said Pippa. *"And . . ."*

"More?"

Yes. The reason she had come to the mountain in the first place: Bas's farm and all the farms around it. "And make sure all the crops are growing well, and no one is suffering. . . ."

"Child, child," said Zeus, putting a hand up to stop her. "Suffering is part of mortal life. Even the gods' lives. But yes, already Demeter is working on the crops and harvests. And as for choice, you will forge your own path, that I can see. That is *all* I can see. We do try to leave mortals to their own devices, you know."

Pippa nodded firmly. She was finished.

Zeus laughed. "And I thought you might not have any wants." He turned to Hero. "And for you, boy?"

Hero hesitated. "There was my father's cloak. . . ."

"This?" said Zeus, pulling it from his robes. His robes seemed to hide everything!

Unlike Pippa's coin, which had grown more beautiful from their adventure, the lion cloak looked worse for wear. It was faded and tattered, and the lion head looked like it was about to fall off.

"I thought of returning this to you, but—and I can change it back to what it once was if you disagree—I think this is so much better."

He shook out the cloak like a sheet of linen and, to Pippa's amazement, as it drifted back down, it transformed. It was no longer a worn-out lion's skin. It was a beautiful himation, a midnight-black cloak embroidered with tiny pictures—stories and symbols so intriguing Pippa wanted to gaze at each one.

Along the bottom edge there was even a picture of two children, a horse, and a hippalektryon as well as other scenes she recognized—them escaping from Morpheus, and Hero tricking Achlys. There were also some she hadn't been a part of—like Hero facing the taraxippoi and freeing the gods and goddesses. The embroidery didn't go all the way around.

The cloak was like the staff of a song-stitcher, a storyteller, with its carvings. Hero reached out a hand and touched it hesitantly. "For me?"

"For you," said Zeus, draping it around him. It fit perfectly. "You will have your whole life to finish it, if you wish. Now what else can I grant you?"

"My family," said Hero. "They have never loved me. I don't want . . . I mean, can I . . ."

"Ah." Zeus shook his head sadly. "I know what you are going to ask. It's not possible, I'm afraid. You are part of your family's very threads. Once a thread is woven, nothing can be done to it, except snipping. I can't help you with your family."

Maybe I *can,* thought Pippa. Could Hero come back with her? She was still becoming part of Bas's family, and she'd caused a lot of trouble already. Not that Hero would be trouble. . . .

Before she could say anything, the faraway voice spoke again. *"Go on, boy! Spit it out!"*

"I didn't finish," Hero said to Zeus. "The Fates, they want me to stay with them. At least for a bit. And Pecklion too. They want me to tell them stories while they work. Plus there are all these tangled threads they need someone to untangle . . . Or was it threads they need me to tangle?"

"Are you sure you want to stay with the Fates?" asked Zeus, raising an eyebrow. "They don't do anyone any favors, you know."

Pippa and Hero exchanged knowing glances. What was the map then? And even the olive soup . . .

Still, Hero said matter-of-factly, "I don't think this is a favor. They *are* grumpy. But grumpy isn't the same as mean. I can handle grumpy."

"But can you handle olive soup?"

"I've always wanted to learn how to cook," said Hero with a smile.

Pippa smiled too. The Fates were the three most magical grandmothers she could imagine. Hero needed love in his life. She had plenty. Bas's family *did* care for her, and of course, there was Tazo. And Zeph! Pippa couldn't wait to get back to him. Would he be surprised to see his colt flying? But Zeph couldn't fly with him. . . .

"Good!" said Zeus, clapping his hands. "All is settled then."

"Actually," said Pippa, "there is one more thing."

"Really?" the great god said.

Pippa stood on tiptoe, and Zeus crouched down, as she whispered her last request in his ear.

He chuckled. "Very well, child. Very well."

Twenty-five

At the Stables of the Seven Sisters, the horses grazed contentedly in the pasture. Their coats gleamed brighter, their tails swished stronger than before. Some said that now, after the salt storm, the grass grew even greener, especially there.

Maybe that was why the wild horses broke down the walls more often than ever.

Pippa sighed as she hoisted a fallen rock back into place. She wiped her hands on her chiton, the one the Fates had made for her. It seemed much more resilient than the map, and even when she cleaned her dirty hands on it, it stayed clean, which made both Pippa and Helena happy.

Not that Helena complained much these days. She and Nikon were so thankful that Pippa and Tazo had helped save the stables, the land . . . Olympus itself. Sometimes Pippa had to remind them how grateful *she* was that they had given her a home—and now, more than that.

Even old Leda was repentant, admitting that Tazo was not to blame and apologizing for jumping to conclusions. Though she *was* still constantly poking her nose in everyone's business. At that very moment, Pippa could see her hobbling toward the old stables, to watch the day's activities.

It must almost be time.

Indeed, just then Bas called out, "Lessons, Pippa! Lessons!"

Pippa lifted the last stone into place, wiped her sweaty hands again, and felt a thrill. Lessons. She looked forward to them every day. Of course, these were very different lessons.

She hurried to the old stables.

It had been transformed into a proper barn again, albeit a small one. One day she might need more space, but for now, it worked fine.

In front of the barn door, a handful of young children had gathered—boys and girls. Some were shyly
shuffling their sandals. Others were so excited they
were bouncing up and down on their toes.

Each week it seemed there were more children.
Still, Pippa made sure everyone got a turn, especially
the foundlings.

"Can I fly on Tazo this time? Please?" begged a boy,
who was missing his front teeth.

"I want to ride too!" declared a girl hopping from
foot to foot.

"Hush, hush," said Pippa with a smile. "You'll get
a chance, but I'm not sure if it will be today. There
is much you need to learn first—safety, bridling, the
proper commands. Now, are you all here?" She took a
quick survey. "Where's Astrea?"

Astrea, Bas's youngest sister, never missed the
lessons.

The boy with the gap teeth pointed up.

Pippa looked. There, soaring into the air, was little
Astrea riding Tazo.

Tazo's wings sparkled in the sunlight.

"Oh, Astrea!" cried Pippa.

Astrea's hair whipped out behind her as she and

Tazo spun up into a cloud and then down again. She was a natural. And so, for that matter, was Tazo. He had really grown into his wings.

Pippa should have been mad. But the sight of them rising into the sky reminded her of someone else, not too long ago. She smiled.

"Zeph!" She blew on the whistle around her neck, and a moment later her horse arrived, galloping in from the pasture. The children gasped. Some had seen Zephyr before. Others hadn't. His massive wings fanned out beside him.

Perhaps he hadn't missed them, but he seemed to enjoy them now that they had returned. Zeus granted her last wish.

Pippa slipped onto his back. She wanted to make sure Astrea was okay. "Fly, Zeph. Petesthe," she whispered. He responded at once. The wind pressed against her cheeks like a kiss.

In the distance, the clouds were rumbling. The gods were up to something. When were they not?

But Pippa didn't mind.

Riding, flying, friends. Her own winged horse stables. She had touched the stars, and the stars had become her dreams.

In the stable built into the cliffs of Mount Olympus, a winged goddess pushed her mop. Her feet were wet and cold. But there was no point in complaining. Besides, the god next to her was doing that well enough already.

"Can't you tie up your cloak? It keeps tripping me!" Poseidon groaned.

"I can't help my cloak, but you can help your feet," retorted Nyx. She wanted to remind him that this particular mess was not her doing. She hadn't filled the winged horse stables with salt water. He had. But again, what was the point? Zeus had commanded that they clean the stables, and so they must.

Both of them were exhausted. Zeus had forbidden the use of magic, which meant all they had were the useless tools of the mortals. Pathetic mops and buckets that made their task never-ending.

Her back hurt; her wings ached. And the stables reeked of rotten fish.

All Nyx longed for was night. Her night.

The girl, the mortal one, had been right after all. Night was wonderful. Finally, at the end of the day, Night meant you could rest your weary head and hands.

At last, the call came. It was time.

Nyx cast her cloak proudly out through the archway.

The stars glittered, the moon shone, and everyone—gods and mortals alike—felt darkness settle over them, sweet and calm and good.

The Katasterismoi:
A Constellation Guide to

the
Horses
of the
Sky

About This Guide

The constellations in Ancient Greece were mostly heroes and beasts favored by the gods and goddesses, who received a place in the stars in honor of their deeds. Semidivine spirits, the constellations could stride across the heavens and were part of the divine cloak of Nyx (goddess of night). These below are the brightest of the star horses.

Pegasus

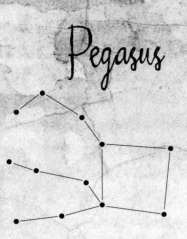

Pegasus was a winged horse born of Poseidon, god of the sea, and Medusa, a winged monster with snake hair. When Pegasus's hooves hit the earthly ground, they created the Hippocrene well. Pegasus was caught by the hero Bellerophon with the help of Athena, goddess of wisdom. Riding Pegasus, Bellerophon accomplished many great feats, including defeating the terrible monster the Chimera. Later, Bellerophon tried to fly up to Mount Olympus on the back of Pegasus and fell off. Afterward, Pegasus became Zeus's steed and helped carry the great god's thunder and lightning bolts. Eventually, Zeus honored Pegasus's exploits by transforming him into a constellation with the help of Nyx. The Pegasus constellation is one of the largest constellations in the sky and lies in the northern hemisphere.

Diokles

Diokles was Zeus's steed following Pegasus, and the winner of the very first Winged Horse Race. The rider and trainer of Diokles, Archippos, still trains winged horses on Mount Olympus to this day. Poseidon was the patron god of them both, also being god of horses. It is no wonder his horse won. Now, Diokles holds a treasured place beside Pegasus.

Ismene

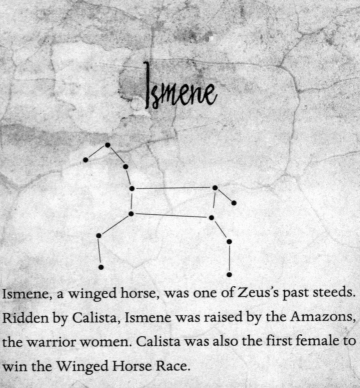

Ismene, a winged horse, was one of Zeus's past steeds. Ridden by Calista, Ismene was raised by the Amazons, the warrior women. Calista was also the first female to win the Winged Horse Race.

Nikomedes

The most recent addition to the night sky, Nikomedes was Zeus's steed before the last Winged Horse Race. Dion was Nikomedes's mortal rider, and Apollo was their patron god. Nikomedes, still rather spritely, is often found galloping across the night sky and mistaken for a shooting star.

Kerauno

This monstrous winged horse is not actually a constellation. However, he is worth a mention. He was Bas's steed in the last Winged Horse Race, and along with Pippa, Zephyr, and Bas, was banished by Zeus to the mortal realm afterward. Unlike the others, he did not obey. Instead, Kerauno took flight, and no one was able to catch him. Now he can sometimes be seen flying high in the heavens—a dark flash like a black comet—as though he wishes he were a constellation.

Hali, Skotos, Khruse

Hali, the ocean-blue horse; Skotos, the black steed; and golden Khruse are three of the hundreds of winged horses temporarily transformed into constellations by Nyx, at the request of Poseidon. Their transformation lasted only moments in the gods' lives, though the horses themselves forever carry a sheen that they didn't have before.

Acknowledgments

The creation of a book is a long and wonderful process that involves, for me, many people to whom I'm forever grateful. I wrote this book while I was pregnant with my son and actually finished it the day before he came—a little early—into the world. It's no wonder we named him after a constellation! So, to my family: my son, husband, and parents. To my writing group, the Inkslingers. To my friend and coteacher, Lee Edward Fodi, and my writing soul mate, Vikki Vansickle. To my fantastic editors, Dave Linker and Lucy Pearse, and the whole teams at their publishing houses. To my amazing agent, Emily van Beek. To the exceptionally talented wordsmith, Tiffany Stone. And to my expert on all things related to ancient Greece, Tom Donaghy. Thank you all, so very much.